T0103768

Mrs. Jones

Mrs. Jones

AHMED ELKASHEF

PARTRIDGE

Copyright © 2016 by Ahmed Elkashef.

ISBN:	Hardcover	978-1-4828-6474-8
	Softcover	978-1-4828-6472-4
	eBook	978-1-4828-6473-1

All rights reserved. No part of this book may be used or reproduced by any means, graphic, electronic, or mechanical, including photocopying, recording, taping or by any information storage retrieval system without the written permission of the author except in the case of brief quotations embodied in critical articles and reviews.

Because of the dynamic nature of the Internet, any web addresses or links contained in this book may have changed since publication and may no longer be valid. The views expressed in this work are solely those of the author and do not necessarily reflect the views of the publisher, and the publisher hereby disclaims any responsibility for them.

Print information available on the last page.

To order additional copies of this book, contact
Toll Free 800 101 2657 (Singapore)
Toll Free 1 800 81 7340 (Malaysia)
orders.singapore@partridgepublishing.com

www.partridgepublishing.com/singapore

Contents

Prologue

A painting bought at an auction in Quebec leads to a very surprising discovery about one of Dr. Oliver's patients. This story is about Helen, an artist with bipolar disorder, and her family and friends who were impacted by her mood cycles.

Based on true-life events, and set in beautiful South Carolina, the story is fast paced and gripping with many twists and turns.

1

Old Times Gallery

The last day of July was hot and muggy in Mt. Pleasant , northern Virginia. Dr. Oliver - a staff psychiatrist at the community mental health center - was an attractive brunette with large glasses and hair that was always unkempt. She was usually very busy in her office. But she was particularly so on this day, as it was the last day before she left for a long weekend to Quebec to celebrate her tenth wedding anniversary.

"Thanks so much Elaine, I really appreciate you covering my patients while I'm gone. I've put in the orders for the medications for everyone who needs refills. Mr. Monahan is coming in two days for his blood work. If you could please check it before he gets his next Clozaril prescription ... anyway Marilyn should remind you. Nothing really major to report: the therapists know what to do and will get in touch with you with any problems," said Dr. Oliver, on a phone call to her colleague Dr. Green.

"Have a great time and don't worry. Make sure you eat at Chez Louise - great food."

Dr. Oliver went back to the pile of medical records on her desk, signing and entering orders in the computer while being repeatedly interrupted by therapists and nurses.

"Don't forget the order for Mrs. Hernandez," said Eleanore. "I'm doing it right now," replied Dr. Oliver. "Mrs. Jones didn't come for her last two appointments and I'm very worried about her, she usually deteriorates really fast. Remember the last time when she took off …"

Dr. Oliver impatiently interrupted, "Yes I do remember. If you guys just leave me alone, I can get a lot done. I'm trying to get out of here. I have a plane to catch in four hours and I'm not even packed yet. Did you try to reach her?"

Jackie interrupted her as she raised her hand. "Ok, ok, don't get short with me sister. Anything I can help with?"

Dr. Oliver smiled. "Can you put an alert in the system and I'll talk with Rose on the way out."

"Ok sweetie have fun, I'm going to leave you alone now. Oh just one more … " and before she had even finished her sentence, she ran out of the door to avoid being hit by a flying stapler.

"Finally, oh my God," Dr. Oliver exhaled as she was signing the last order. She quickly gathered her stuff in her three handbags and bolted out of the door. She suddenly stopped as she remembered that she had forgotten to talk with Rose.

"Oh shit - Mrs. Jones," she mumbled to herself and ran back quickly to the ER.

"Hi Rose."

"You're still here?" Rose replied.

"Yep and I need to run, quickly. Mrs. Jones hasn't shown up for her last two appointments. She's out of meds I'm sure. She may be brought in by the police like last time."

"Did you put an alert in the system?" asked Rose.

"Yes, Jackie's doing it."

"Do you want us to send mobile?"

"You know, it may not be a bad idea. Can you please discuss it with Jackie. I've got to run," Dr. Oliver replied as she walked away.

"Ok, go have fun," said Rose.

Melissa Oliver got in her car and zoomed off.

"Hi, I'm home."

"Hi Honey, I'm up here," answered Bob, who was finishing packing upstairs. She ran upstairs and stopped at the door of their bedroom.

"Oh you packed for me too. You are amazing."

She gave her husband a big hug and a kiss.

"I packed all your sexy underwear, garments and the torture stuff, belts and all." He opened her suitcase as he was talking to show her.

"You're going to be tortured really bad," she said, making a heavy grunting sound, as she groped and bit him on the neck. "Don't forget your Viagra pills!" she added.

"Oh shoot, I am out!" said Bob going along with the joke.

"Not to worry, I picked up some samples from the clinic," replied Melissa.

"Oh, you are bad - and good," said Bob.

Melissa laughed, looked at her watch and said, "Oh God, we have to leave now or we'll miss the flight!"

They closed the bags in a hurry and made a mad rush to the door.

"Oh the passports!" remembered Bob,

"Do we need passports to go to Canada?" asked Melissa.

"Now we do."

The traffic to Regan Airport was heavy as usual. They made it just in time to park the car and rush to the gate. After they were checked in, Melissa buckled her seatbelt, held Bob's hand, took a deep breath and closed her eyes.

"Wake me up when we get there."

"Will do," said Bob.

A couple of hours later, they arrived in Quebec and took a cab to their favorite hotel Le Château Frontenac, where they had spent their honeymoon. This was their tenth anniversary and they wanted to re-live their honeymoon. They booked the same suite and worked out a very detailed program of the places they had visited and the restaurants they had eaten at, and of course the galleries. They both loved art and they own a small art collection.

As they walked into the hotel lobby, Melissa shouted, "I've got to go to the girl's room." Bob did not hear her. He was totally absorbed, looking at a painting on the wall. It was a portrait of a pretty woman which reminded him of the first painting he inherited from his grandmother. He was having a flashback of his grandmother yelling at him when she caught him touching the girl's face in the painting.

"Don't ever touch this painting again! As a matter of fact, don't touch *any* painting. You can ruin it with your hands."

His grandmother had been getting very sick around the time he visited her. "I know how much you loved that painting and I want you to have it so you can remember me."

"Grandma is that you in the painting?" asked Bob, who was shocked to hear this.

Grandma took a deep breath and looked at the window. She stared into space as if she was remembering something.

"Yes, it is me. It is a long story Bobby."

Then she let out a sigh. Grandma kept quiet for few seconds as if she was making up her mind whether to divulge her lifelong secret. She needed to let it out. She could not imagine with her frail health that she would go to her grave without someone knowing the truth. Who was more deserving to share it with than her grandson?

"I used to date an artist before I met your grandfather. He's the one who painted that portrait of me."

Bob could see her eyes filling with tears. A tear came down her cheek.

"Grandma you're crying. What happened to him?" asked Bob.

"Oh, he killed himself. Something was wrong with him. He was very moody. One day he was happy and so much fun to be around. The next he was as miserable as could be. I couldn't stand him when he got that way. I left him many times but ..." she paused.

"But what Grandma?"

She looked at him and said, "Bob, promise me you won't tell anyone about this."

Bob looked very nervous about what he was about to hear. "I promise grandma."

"I was pregnant." She paused, looking at her grandson's face. "I was pregnant with your mother when I married your grandfather. He didn't know. No one knew. He thought Helen was his child. I couldn't tell him, in fact I couldn't tell anybody. In those days it was such a shame to have a child out of wedlock. I was going to marry Otto when I found out, but he ended up killing himself." She was still staring into space, but felt relieved to finally let her secret out. "Now I can die in peace Bobby."

She looked into her grandson's eyes and held his hands.

"I wanted you to know, so maybe one day you will find your mother."

He looked back at her, confused. As if she read his mind, she answered, "Yes, you can tell her."

*

"Are we done daydreaming?" Melissa said, trying to get Bob's attention. He had not noticed her return. He smiled back and gave her a hug. They checked into their suite and decided to stay in for the night.

They had dinner at Le Champlaine, the elegant French restaurant at the hotel.

"If you have escargot, I won't sleep with you," said Melissa. They both loved French food, but escargot was where Melissa drew the line. The thought of eating snails made her stomach turn, and the thought of kissing someone who had just eaten snails was too repulsive.

After dinner, they went back to their suite and made passionate love. Melissa said, "I don't think you're going to need Viagra any more!"

Bob, imitating Ronald Regan's voice, replied, "Well, well, young lady, you should trust but verify!"

"What, you took a pill?"

Bob laughed.

"So what is on tap for tomorrow?" Melissa answered as she was dozing off.

"We'll figure it out then."

"Good night my love."

"Good night Doc." And they both called it a night.

Bob got up early in the morning and as usual turned on the TV and started making coffee. The noise woke up Mellisa as he was hoping it would.

"Oh I feel great, I slept like a baby," said Melissa.

"Me too. This bed is so comfortable," Bob replied as he was checking the mattress. "Uhm, Sweet Dreams - never heard of that brand."

"I had a nice dream," replied Melissa. "I dreamed that I was nursing a beautiful little girl. She looked at me with her beautiful big green eyes, stopped feeding, and said, 'Hi my name is Helen, what's your name?' As I was about to answer, I saw you sucking on my other breast looking very content. I wonder what it means."

"Well, I'm always content when I suck on your breasts - so that part is easy to figure out. Besides, you're the shrink, but I can offer my own interpretation if you like. I'm sure it has to do with what we did last night," replied Bob, reaching for her breast.

"Stop it, that is just too obvious."

"I feel there's some kind of connection with you and the baby," said Melissa.

"You mean, because her name is Helen like my mother's? Oh God that is creepy, me and my mom are sucking on your boppies!"

"I wonder where Helen is? Do you think she's alive somewhere?" asked Melissa.

"Ahhh, I'd give everything I own to find out," said Bob, his face looked sad.

"I'm sorry ..." Melissa felt guilty for changing his mood.

"It's ok," replied Bob.

"So what's on tap for today?" asked Melissa, trying to change the subject. "I feel like having a huge breakfast then going for a walk."

"Sounds good to me."

They ordered breakfast in the room.

"They still have the crab crepe on the menu - I can't believe it. remember?"

"I sure do. I still remember me trying to say it in French."

"I'm afraid you have to do it again."

"No problem Sugar - for you, anything," said Bob, as he was trying to spread Melissa's legs.

"Not now. After breakfast!"

Bob grabbed the phone and ordered, "Dou crepe crab sil vous pla."

"Sorry sir, I did not understand. You can say it in English. I do speak English."

"No, I'm not going to say it in English. I think I spoke very clear French. Doo crab crepe for two. I mean: two stuffed crepe with crab pour doou. Got that?"

Melissa was about to fall off the edge of the bed from laughing.

"Sir, please, I'll be glad to come to the room to take your order."

"Don't come to the room. I am speaking in perfect clear French. Where are you from? Do you speak French?"

"Yes sir. I was born in Bordeaux."

"Ah, so you are not from around here?"

"Sir, please. I have others calling on the other lines. I need to hang up."

"Don't you dare hang up!"

Melissa grabbed the phone, "We're very sorry sir, my husband was trying to impress me with his French, please excuse us."

"No problem madam, what would you like for breakfast?"

"Two crab crepes, orange juice and coffee."

"Right away madam."

The weather couldn't have been better: 60 degrees, sunny and fresh. Melissa exhaled as she took her first deep breath outside.

"Oh my God this is perfect." She looked at the sky and said, "Thank you."

They started walking down the old city toward St. Louis Gate and from there to St. Paul Street, stopping at the antique dealers' district. They both loved antiques. They decided to stop there for lunch to do some treasure hunting.

"You could have gotten it for much less if you'd tried haggling," commented Bob on the little statute of Freud that Melissa bought for 38 dollars.

"I think it's cute. Besides, I felt bad for the old lady."

"Oh, what's that?" asked Melissa, pointing to the bag Bob was holding.

"Oh, it's a surprise."

"Ah, can I see it please?"

"Later tonight maybe, if you're a good girl."

"Again? We just did it this morning!" exclaimed Melissa.

"Oh well, I think I'm getting the vacation libido surge."

"Is that a new psychiatric condition?"

"I guess. Any two of the following criteria: elevated mood, increased desire to have sex, and craving for seafood," said Bob.

Melissa laughed. "I guess you have the first two. No more crab crepes for you."

After lunch, they continued walking around the old city. They both stopped suddenly at the Old Times Gallery, looking at the big sign on the door: *Going out of business - auction today.* They looked at each other and walked in. They were greeted by the owner who introduced himself as Guy.

"Welcome. Please come in."

"Thank you. Business isn't good these days it seems."

"I'm afraid so madam: it's the economy. Also, we specialize in old classical art. Everybody's into modern art these days, I guess."

"Well, we're not," answered Bob.

"Oh great, please have a look around. The auction starts very soon."

There were few people looking at the paintings on the walls. Melissa stopped at a painting of an old man with a baby girl sitting in his lap. "I like this painting it is very cute and kind of unusual - you usually see a mother and a child."

"Yes, it is cute," said Bob, appearing in a pensive mood as if trying to remember something. "The guy reminds me of someone, but I can't think who."

"Interested?" asked Melissa

"Let's see how it goes. If the price is right — sure, why not?" Bob looked around as if sizing up the competition.

"Ladies and gentlemen, please take your seats. My name is Allan La Roche. I am with Emille's auction house. Today, we'll be selling everything in the gallery. Let me remind you of the rules. Your bid is a contract. If you raise your number that means you are interested in bidding. The bidding increments are 100 for the first 1000, then 500 for the first 5000, then 1000 thereafter."

The auction started with few landscapes that went for very low prices. Bob and Melissa got excited about the chance of grabbing the painting they wanted for a very low price.

"Next is painting of a father, or possibly a grandfather, and a child. Very unusual oil painting signed H.B. Jones, New York. We think this is the famous American artist Hugh Bolton Jones. We are opening the bidding for 20,000 dollars."

Bob and Melissa looked at each other in surprise.

"Wow! Twenty grand to start!" Bob was already on his iPad checking the Internet for Hugh Bolton Jones. "I thought so: no way this is a Hugh Bolton Jones. The guy painted trees most of his career. Funny, he is from Baltimore and his largest collection is at Baltimore Art Museum," he mumbled.

Minutes passed and no one raised their numbers.

"10,000 ... 5000 ... 1000 ..."

The auctioneer kept on lowering the opening bid. Finally, at 1000, Melissa raised her hand. Bob looked at her, not sure if this was such a good idea, but did not say anything.

"1000, looking for 1500 ... 1500 looking for 2000 ..."

Melissa raised her hand again.

"What is your limit?" Bob whispered in her ear. She made a hand gesture for him to stop.

"Looking for 2500 ... 2500 once ... twice ... gone for 2000 for number 117! Congratulations. Great buy!" said the auctioneer. They waited for a while, watching the sales. Then they decided to walk some more and collect their painting on the way back.

At the hotel room after a long day, Bob said, "Boy I'm exhausted, we must have walked ten miles or more today."

"Yeah, good exercise," replied Melissa.

"Interested in foot massage?" asked Bob.

"Sure, will that cost me?"

"Yep the usual."

"I thought you were tired?"

"Oh not that tired."

"The vacation libido thing still going on?"

"You got it Doc!"

"If that continues, I may have to put you on medication."

"Really, what would that be?"

"Oh not to worry, we have a lot of medicines that can cure that."

Bob started working on her feet.

"Oh, where did you get the oil?"

"That's the surprise. I found it at the antique market. It's supposed to be an aphrodisiac emulsion from ancient Egypt. It's 5000 years old and made from sandalwood."

"Really?"

"Yeah, it's more expensive than the painting you bought today."

"Oh I feel so special, I feel like Cleopatra."

"You should."

As she was relaxing more and more, Bob kept massaging higher and higher up her legs, then her thighs.

"Ok, it's working!" she surrendered.

2

Mount Pleasant Community Center ER

Back at the community mental health center, two police cars pulled in front of the ER. There was a highly agitated, very disheveled lady in her sixties, in the back of the car. She was handcuffed. Once she got out, she started thrashing around. She was dressed in a white wedding dress that had turned gray from the dirt it had collected over time. Her dress was torn in many places, including the bust area and her hips, showing most of her legs. Some of the rips looked intentional. From the way she smelled, one could tell that she had not showered for some time. She had been wearing this dress for days, if not weeks.

"Mrs. Jones calm down please," said Matt, the mental health specialist who was on duty that night.

Mrs. Jones was very well known to all the community mental health centers within a 100-mile radius and to the police departments as well.

"What happened this time?" One could tell from the way Matt asked the police officer, that somehow he knew the answer already.

"We caught her on Highway One. She was standing in the middle of the traffic exposing herself to the public and asking if anyone wanted to marry her."

"I didn't ask you to marry me, you son of a bitch! I wouldn't marry you even if you were the last man on earth. I'm Queen Sheba! You know how many kings and knights are out there? It's like night and day. Daydream as much as you like, I'll never marry you. You'll see what I'll do with you. I'm going to order them to cut you into two thousand, four hundred and fifty pieces. Even King Solomon won't be able to put you back together. Humpty Dumpty, you know that? I command you! Hey you!" Looking at another staff passing by, "Hey you come back here - this is Queen Sheba talking to you. Kneel! You too: I'll cut you into five thousand pieces. You listen to me!"

She became distracted by another member of staff who happened to come out of an interview room.

"What's your name? Hey look!" She bent forward to show her breasts. "You want to suck on these honey? Come back here, these are Queen Sheba's breasts. They are the best. Whatever you like: I got milk, I got hot chocolate - better than Starbucks and it's free. Come back. I will marry you. I command you to propose! Make me an offer. I'm the richest woman in the world. I got money, I got sex, unlimited - both unlimited."

Matt was writing down his observations and assessment, but he needed to ask her a few questions, so he tried to interrupt.

"Mrs. Jones, can I ask you few questions?"

"Shut the fuck up, I did not give you permission to speak. I'm the queen. I'll cut you into seven thousands pieces. Guards! Guards!"

She was calling so loud that many staff from the neighboring offices and the center security rushed to the ER to see if they could help.

"Come on, take them. This one, this one and this one."

She was pointing to Matt and the two police officers.

"Cut them up and throw away the pieces. Now, two thousand, five thousand and seven ..."

Again, Matt tried to interrupt.

"Mrs. Jones, please!"

Rose, the psychiatrist on duty, came out of her office.

"This isn't going to work. We need to admit her - can you call 3A." Then, looking at the police officer. "You'll have to be the petitioner."

"No problem," replied the officer, who was obviously getting exasperated, and was rushing to attend to other calls.

"I'm not going to any hospitals, I'm telling you. I refuse!" said the agitated patient.

"We need to admit you for your safety and the safety of the public. You were endangering your own life and the lives of people on the highway. Obviously you stopped taking your medication."

"I don't need your stinking medication. There's nothing wrong with me. I refuse, you can't force me to take it! Uncuff me now, I command you, I'm getting out of here."

"You can't Mrs. Jones. You're going to the hospital to be treated."

She suddenly lunged at the police officer, who stepped back quickly. Looking at Matt, he asked "Can't you guys give her something?"

Matt looked at Dr. Rose who nodded affirmatively. He left to get the Haldol and Ativan injections. The officers held her while Matt gave her the shot.

"You're going to jail, I'm going to sue you and you. I'm going to sue all of you. You bastards!" she yelled.

Matt made the call. Luckily, there was a bed available at the 3A psychiatric ward at Mt. Pleasant hospital across the street. He quickly finished the paperwork and handed it to the officer.

The police officers took her back into the car and drove across the street to the hospital ER where the admitting psychiatric nurse was waiting for them.

"Welcome back Mrs. Jones."

Mrs Jones was getting less agitated by that time.

"What's for dinner Jackie?" she asked, recognizing a familiar face.

"We have your favorite - fish and chips."

"Oh good, but I'm not staying after dinner."

"Ok let's go talk about it."

3

Mt. Pleasant Hospital Psychiatric Ward

Mrs. Jones was escorted to the ward and put in the constant observation room. She was becoming more cooperative, allowing the nurse to check her.

"Your vital signs are normal Mrs. Jones," said the nurse.

"I already told you people: there's nothing wrong with me!"

After dinner, they started her back on her medication.

"What is that?"

"Seroquel"

"I don't want it."

"But it will help you sleep."

She looked the other way in refusal.

"Please," said Jackie.

"Your Majesty," said Mrs. Jones.

"Sorry?"

"Please, *Your Majesty.*"

"Please, Your Majesty," said Jackie, smiling.

Jackie and Mrs. Jones went back a long way. Jackie knew her through her repeated admissions to Mt. Pleasant over the years. She always liked Mrs. Jones and Mrs. Jones liked her back and trusted her. This kind of relationship between a doctor, or a nurse, and their patient was sacred. It was miraculous that in the midst of all the agitation, delusions and the psychosis that patients went through, they could trust and follow the advice of certain staff. Somehow they knew that what they are going through was abnormal and had to be stopped.

Mrs. Jones slept for two days from exhaustion. The staff went in to check on her at regular times to give her medication, and ask her if she wanted to eat. But they left her to rest in between, which was mostly what she needed.

On the third day of her admission, at her scheduled commitment hearing, the police officer and the treating doctor were there pushing for her continued involuntary admission.

"What have we here?" asked Judge Harrison.

"Mrs. Jones, Your Honor."

"Oh no, not again. What did she do this time?"

"It's the same story Your Honor: she stopped her medication and relapsed," proceeded Dr. Wolf, while looking at the police officer to add more details.

"Your Honor we found her on Highway One in the middle of traffic, exposing herself to male drivers and asking if someone would propose to her."

"Any accidents?"

"No sir, thank God, but almost. It's a miracle we didn't have a pile of cars on the highway. She herself almost got struck many times."

"We hope the court allows us to keep her for treatment until she's stable," added Dr. Wolf.

The judge then looked at Mr. Lewis, the court-appointed attorney, for rebuttal.

"Doctor can't you treat her as an outpatient?" asked Mr. Lewis. However, the way he asked the question implied that he asked it only for the record, otherwise he was totally convinced that she needed to be in the hospital.

"She was being treated as an outpatient, but she is non-compliant with her medication. She doesn't think she has any problem and she certainly doesn't want to take medication."

The judge, having dealt with hundreds of similar cases, intervened. Looking at the doctor, he said, "I'm really tired of this. This is so much money and time wasted here - taxpayers' money, my time, our time. How are we going to deal with this, so we don't have this revolving door business? I'm tired of hearing about patients not compliant with their treatment. *Make* them compliant!" he was clearly getting exasperated.

"Your Honor, if you tell us to treat them involuntarily we will," answered the doctor.

"It is your job to treat them and figure out a way to keep them *in* treatment."

"Our hands are tied Your Honor. We can't force treatment on anyone who refuses if they are no harm to themselves or others."

"I don't want to see her in my court again. Give her the proper treatment. If she needs long-term treatment, you can transfer her to the state hospital," said the judge, while signing the commitment papers.

The judge knew exactly what Dr. Wolf was referring to: the issue of a patient's right to refuse treatment unless they were a clear danger to themselves or others. The issue of treating patients in a least restrictive environment, created a dilemma to mental health professionals and the police. Many patients who were roaming the streets homeless and talking to themselves would not be treated unless there was an imminent danger. 'Imminence' was a very confusing word and most of the time no one was there at the right time when things were 'imminent'. Most of the time, the danger had already happened before patients were brought for treatment. There was no clear and fast fix for the situation. Both the judge or the doctor knew it.

*

By the fourth day, Mrs. Jones was doing much better. She was calmer, and cleaner, and she agreed to join the 'drop in' group.

"Guess who's back with us?" said Jackie, who was leading the session. A few of the patients knew Mrs. Jones, and their faces lit up.

"Hi, Mrs. Jones."

She waved with her right hand, looking tired and sleepy.

"I know you're still tired, so if you don't feel like sharing anything with the group today we understand."

Jackie looked at the others in the group, as if to get their agreement. They all nodded approvingly. There were five patients in the room: they were all sitting in a circle discussing their mental illness, coping with it and their treatment. Mrs. Jones started talking in a tired, low voice with her eyes barely open.

"Why do I have to take this awful medicine that makes me sleepy and tired all the time? I hate it."

"Does anyone want to answer Mrs. Jones?"

Jackie looked at the other group members.

"You have a chemical imbalance and the medicine will help you to fix it," answered George, a schizophrenic patient who had been on medication on and off for a long time.

"I don't have a chemical imbalance, you idiot. There's nothing wrong with me."

"Mrs. Jones, that's not nice," Jackie interrupted.

George looked hurt.

"Please apologize to George. He was only trying to help."

"I am Queen Sheba. I don't apologize to anyone."

She was dozing off again, as she spoke very slowly.

"I think Mrs. Jones isn't ready yet for the group. Please excuse me while I take her back to her room."

"Yeah she isn't ready, take her away," nodded Steve, a patient with severe obsessive compulsive disorder.

Jackie walked back into the room, trying to get the group back on track.

"So George, you were saying something before Mrs. Jones walked in - about the TV?"

"Yes they invented a color TV."

"Can you tell us more about that observation, or what is the point you're trying to tell the group?"

"That *is* my point: they invented a color TV," repeated George.

"You must have been watching TV every day for the last twenty years. You just noticed it is in color today?" commented Steve.

George looked bewildered, as if realizing the impact of what he had just said.

"George that is a very interesting insight. I also noticed that you're interacting more with other patients."

George smiled back in agreement, but did not exactly know how to explain it.

"Do you think it is the new medication?"

George was labeled 'treatment resistant' and spent most of his life in state hospitals. Three weeks previously, he was put on Clozaril, a last-resort medication to treat schizophrenia.

"I like the new medicine, I just don't like the blood work."

"I know George, no one likes needles. But it's for your own good," replied Jackie.

"I know. It's ok I guess."

"Can I try it too?" asked Maggie a 20-year-old borderline patient, who was admitted following a suicide attempt.

"Nothing seems to work for me. I still feel like I want to kill myself," she said, looking at her bandaged wrists.

"I'm sorry you aren't feeling well, Maggie," said Jackie. "You can certainly discuss with your doctor if this is an appropriate medication for you. But we all need to remember that medication, although a very important part of the treatment, is not the only thing. We do need to learn to understand ourselves better, and our problems - especially the ones that keep happening over and over and over. We need to learn better ways of coping with our frustration and stress."

"Labla, labla, lab, la," said Maggie.

"I know you heard it before, but that is what we have to do to get better."

"Coping my ass! I've been coping for twenty years and look where it got me!" said Michael, an alcoholic and drug addict who had been struggling with his addiction for years.

"You sound frustrated," Jackie commented.

"You bet I am. I've been in treatment all my life. Every time I think I'm pulling myself out, I'm pulled back in."

"It sounds to me that you are really angry at yourself Michael for relapsing."

"I am," said the teary-eyed Michael. "I am. I should have called my sponsor. I knew it before I walked into that bar. I knew better than that. It is hard, it is constant, non-stop. You are fighting that voice inside that tells you: 'Go ahead, take a drink. It will be ok, one drink won't hurt you. You can stop whenever you want.' And the other voice that tells you: 'No don't, you're going to regret it. I shouldn't, God damn it!' I was doing really good. I was getting my life back together. I got my driver's license, I had a job. Now it's all gone."

"Michael, addiction is … " Jackie started to speak.

But Michael interrupted and finished her sentence.

"… a chronic relapsing brain disease."

"But you came here on your own. You realized you needed treatment. Next time maybe you can stop and listen to the voice that tells you not to drink. But these episodes are going to continue to happen. You're right: it is a constant battle. But you're not alone fighting it. Use the system and the support you have in place."

"I know Jackie, I know," said Michael raising his hand, as if to say, 'you're not telling me something new.'

"It's almost time to wrap this session up. Does anyone have any final thoughts or quick comments?" asked Jackie, who got no response. It appeared that everyone was ready for a break following Michael's display of emotion.

*

A few days later, Mrs. Jones was getting much better, she was more alert and less delusional. Jackie decided it was time to discuss her long-term treatment plan, since they couldn't keep her on the ward much longer.

"It's been almost ten days since you arrived, and we need to discuss next treatment plans."

"Ok, discuss!" replied Mrs. Jones. "I'm ready to go home."

"You're doing a lot better, but we don't think you're ready to go home," replied Jackie.

"Why is that?" asked Mrs. Jones, starting to get angry.

"Because of your history of not showing up for your outpatient appointments, and not taking your medication, and ending up in the hospital. Your treatment team, and the judge at the hearing, all think that you need to go to long-term hospitalization at the state hospital."

"No, please don't send me there. I'll take my medicine, I promise. I need to go home."

"Where is home?"

"I have a section 8 apartment near King's Street. I'll lose it if you put me in the state hospital. Do you know how long it took to get it? Please Jackie, I'll do whatever you want. Give me the shot. I'll take the shot will that be good?"

"Ok, I don't promise anything, but I'll discuss it with the team to switch you to the shot. You also need to go to the day program across the street. We'll discuss it with your outpatient doctor as a condition for your release. Who's your doctor?"

"Dr. Oliver."

"Ok, if you miss one appointment for your shot, the mobile unit will be sent to get you. If they can't find you, and you end up at the ER again, you'll be sent directly to the state hospital for a very long time, no questions asked. We will not take you again. Clear?" said Jackie.

"Yes madam."

The next day Mrs. Jones was discharged home with clear instructions regarding her medication and her follow-up appointment with Dr. Oliver. She was given her first shot and some clean clothes from the donated clothes bank at the hospital. She started walking back home. On her way, she stopped at the 7-Eleven and picked up some cigarettes, a bag of toast, eggs and a greasy cheese roll.

"God, I can't believe how hungry this medicine is making me! I could eat all the time," she mumbled to the cashier, who did not really seem to care. "Where am I going to get money just to buy food? I must have gained 20 pounds since they put me on the stupid medicine."

4

Back at the Center

Back from vacation, Dr. Oliver walked into her office carrying her usual three handbags and the painting she had bought from Quebec.

"Welcome back, how was it?" asked Rose.

"Oh it was great, but of course very short."

"Anything happen while I was gone?"

"Yeah, Mrs. Jones showed up as expected. We admitted her across the street."

"I'm not surprised, I'll speak with Eleanor about her. Thanks Rose, I got you guys some chocolates."

She pulled a box of chocolates from her bag and handed them over before walking away. She unlocked her door, while looking at a couple of sticky notes that were on the door. She stepped on many papers that had been slipped under her door as she entered her office. She put her bags on the chair, and looked around at the walls for an appropriate place to hang her painting. She put it up, then stepped back few steps to admire it. She smiled with satisfaction. As she was doing this, Michael the team leader walked in.

"Oh hi, you're back! How was it?"

"We had great time!"

"I see you bought a painting."

"Yeah, do you like it?."

"It's unusual. Whatever happened to not hanging pictures in a shrink's office?"

"Oh, those were the good old days of psychoanalysis. We don't do that any more. Besides, it *is* kind of out of the way."

"You heard about Mrs. Jones coming to the ER last week?"

"Yeah, Yeah, Rose told me. I guess we'll discuss it at the team meeting."

"Yeah see you at nine."

The team meetings were at nine o'clock on Mondays for the staff to communicate and discuss treatment issues and new cases. The meeting room was full as usual. The table was covered with goodies: cakes, chocolates and fruits. This was a nice way to start the week and ease into work.

"How was Quebec?" asked several staff, almost at the same time, when Dr. Oliver walked in.

"It was great. We walked, had great food and … " She bashfully smiled.

"I notice baby girl, that you look happy," said a staff member.

"Oh, and I noticed there were three Viagra pills missing from the medication sample supply," said Sarah, the head nurse.

Everyone chuckled.

"Ok people," said Mike, to start business.

"Eleanor: why don't you give us an update on Mrs. Jones."

"Yeah ok, she was discharged yesterday from Mt. Pleasant," looking at Dr. Oliver "She has an appointment with you Wednesday and I'm going to refer her to the day program for screening."

"That's a good idea," said Dr. Oliver.

"By the way, she was switched to the injectable medication. So we need to get her on the schedule with you." She looked at nurse Mitchel who coordinated the 'depot' clinic as it was called.

"Yeah, no problem. I'll put her on the schedule as soon as I get the referral from you."

She looked at Dr. Oliver, who was writing notes in her book.

"Will do," said Dr. Oliver.

"Ok, what else?" asked Mike.

"Steve is also getting ready to be discharged from 3-A. We need to send him to New Beginning. ..."

"I have very sad news," said Chantal who was noticeably quiet. "Mr. Sullivan killed himself over the weekend."

"Oh my God, what happened?"

"He was supposed to spend a weekend with the lady he met recently, but she stood him up last minute. He jumped in front of the metro in DC."

"Oh my God, I heard about it in the local news. But they didn't know the identity."

"Oh he was doing really, really, good."

"When is the funeral?"

"I'll find out and let you know. I was going to go, are you?".

"Definitely," answered the teary- eyed Green.

Mr. Sullivan had been her patient for years. He was a high-functioning schizophrenic, who was doing really well, but he was very sensitive to rejection. He had wanted very badly to have a relationship, but without much luck. No one thought he would end up killing himself.

The meeting ended on this sad note. After the meeting, some staff headed to their offices, and some to the waiting area to get their patients.

"The satellites are still tracking me, and the FBI and the CIA are after me. You got to talk to them. You know what, I think you work for the CIA. What did you say your name was? said Dr. Oliver's new patient.

Mr. Morrisky was a six feet tall, with long and straight blond hair. He was wearing makeup, including bright red lipstick.

"If it makes any difference, I can assure you I don't work for the CIA. Can you tell me what made you move from Las Vegas to Virginia?"

"I came here to have a sex-change operation. They won't do it there. That crazy doctor said I don't need one and she kicked me out of her office. I need you to give me a letter stating that I have to have one. I already started the first part."

"What is that?" asked Dr. Oliver.

"I cut off my penis. Do you want to see?"

"No thanks."

"I've been taking hormones for two years now. See my breasts – they're bigger than yours."

Mr. Morrisky lifted up his t-shirt to show his chest.

"Why do you think you need a sex change operation?" asked Dr. Oliver.

"It's the only way so they can't find me. See - can you feel the satellite? It's here in the room. They're coming for me. I'm out of here!"

Mr. Morrisky was getting more and more agitated. He got up and bolted out of the office. Dr. Oliver called the front desk to let them know, so they could page the team leader. Mike heard the page and called Dr. Oliver's office.

"Are you all right?" asked Mike.

"Mr. Morrisky left my office," said Dr. Oliver.

"I know, I saw him leaving. I was in the front getting my next client. Don't worry, he'll be back."

Later in the evening, it was time for the groups. The AA group and the anger management group members showed up for their meetings at seven o'clock. In the waiting area, they usually shared their therapeutic experiences.

"So, Steve, what step are you at?" asked Bob.

He was a big guy with tattoos all over his body, five earrings in each ear lobe, and a bunch of long necklaces of skulls and five-pointed stars some with red rubies in the center.

"Step three," answered Steve.

He was a mid-forties thin Caucasian male with glasses. He was trying to read his book, before being interrupted by Bob.

"I couldn't make it past step two, man. I was so angry at God. Actually I'm still angry at him."

"So how long have you been sober?"

"It would have been a week, had I not had that drink yesterday."

"I know man, it's hard."

"How are you doing with the anger stuff?" asked Steve.

"I'm not doing shit man. I'm still angry as hell. This is just me, my biology. This is how God made me. I'm very angry at him too. I'm worshiping Satan these days," said Bob touching his necklaces. "We'll see what the fuck he's going to do for me."

"How long have you been in the group?" asked Steve.

"Almost three months now."

"That isn't good."

"I know, it's all bullshit. I'm just doing it because the fucking judge said I have to, otherwise I'm fine, man. I just need to get me another girlfriend, I guess. The bitch gets on my nerves man, she pushes my buttons."

"Why don't you leave her?"

"It's hard man, I'm not working these days. She pays the rent and stuff. I can put up with some shit, but she just nags and nags, non-stop. I just pushed her against the wall, nothing serious. Since she started therapy man, she comes home and talks about assertive shit. She called the police on me. I almost killed her man I swear. Anyway, that's how I ended up here."

"Take care," said Bob.

"Hang in there man," said Steve, as they each walked to their group meetings.

"So Bob, how did it go with Marlene last week?" asked Sam, the group leader.

"Pretty good actually. I almost punched her in the face yesterday, but I didn't. I told her I needed time out and walked outside for few minutes till I was calm."

"Very good. Then what happened?"

"I walked back in and she started nagging me again. I asked her to change the subject. She wouldn't, so I put my fist in the wall and she stopped nagging me."

"What do others think of how Bob reacted?" asked Sam to the group.

"It works," said one group member.

"You got to leave that bitch man," said another.

"Still need treatment - three more months for you," said another.

Bob reacted by making a fist and saying, "Step outside asshole."

Sam had to intervene.

"Calm down everyone. Bob you still exhibited a very angry intimidating reaction to deal with your girlfriend's nagging."

"You try to live with that bitch man, and I guarantee you in two days you will be smacking her. Mr. Wise Man and you will be sitting here with us."

Bob put his hand on the chair next to him. He then looked around the room as if to garner support from the others.

"Bob, you always blame others for your anger. You did the same when you were living with your parents, and the same when you lived with your other roommates. Do you see a common denominator here?"

"Yeah it's them!" He laughed loudly. "Ha ha ha."

"Until you really realize that you have an anger problem, you'll never change."

"Ok, can you pick on someone else now Mr. Wise Ass?" He mumbled the last word very faintly while looking the other way so he wouldn't be heard.

Meanwhile in the other room the AA group was meeting.

"I'm having tough time with this," said Steve. "I drank yesterday. I'm agnostic and I'm not sure where to go with the higher power thing or who to turn to. Honestly, isn't this like saying, 'This isn't my fault, God made me this way and he's supposed to make it go away'?"

"You don't have to be religious to do the twelve steps Steve," commented Colleen, the group leader. "The higher power could be universal energy, a super conscious, collective spirit, whatever you like it to be. Many atheists and agnostics complete the twelve-step program."

"Ok thanks Colleen. I'll do some research and let you know."

Mike was in his office meeting with the McCanns.

"Junior was not doing marijuana. They found marijuana in the car, but it wasn't his," said Mr. McCann, a very heavy-set white male in his mid-fifties, dressed in a blue jeans and a flannel shirt. He was referring to his son who was arrested for possession while driving with his friend two days previously.

"He does. He smokes it every night! I can smell it in his room - you just don't want to believe it. He told me that he likes it. He said it relaxes him and it helps his ADHD," said Mrs. McCann, an overweight attractive blonde in her mid forties.

"You don't know what you're talking about!" said Mr. McCann angrily.

"I think you are in denial here. Listen to your wife. Junior admitted to her that he likes marijuana. If this is his first offense the judge will probably send him to treatment. You need to be supportive and understanding because he is probably scared of how you might react." Said Mike.

"How about Lynn? What are we going to do about her?" asked Mr. McCann, attempting to change the subject to his 19-year-old daughter.

"What about Lynn?" asked Mike.

"She's pregnant."

"Again?"

"Yep, the same guy."

"So you're going to have another baby in the house?"

"Yes, there will be seven of us living in two bedrooms. And he just lost his job," said Mrs. McCann looking at her husband. "My health is very bad. I can't stand for a long time. I have high blood pressure, arthritis, diabetes, and sleep napnia."

"You mean apnea," corrected Mike.

"Yeah that. My family doctor said I need to file for disability - can you help me?"

"I can give you the names of some disability lawyers you can contact."

"Thank you," said Mr. McCann.

"How about you, Mrs. McCann, do you have a job?"

"No, she can't work. She is taking care of us. Without her, we would all fall apart," replied Mr. McCann, who was trying to make amends with his wife.

"Nice try! Falling apart more than *this*? What else could happen?" asked Mrs. McCann, who then added, "He probably wants to sleep with me tonight." She looked at him as if to say, 'I'm on to you.'

Mr. McCann smiled at her, and turned to Mike.

"Do you think Dr. Oliver can give me some Viagra samples before we leave?"

Mike smiled.

"why don't you ask her," he said.

It was getting close to nine o'clock. Everyone was busy writing their final notes of the day and taking charts back to the record room. The cleaning crew was in for end-of-the-day cleaning up.

"Good night everyone," said Dr. Green as she walked past the front desk on her way out.

"Good night Dr. Green," answered the receptionist.

5

Dr. Oliver's Office

It was Wednesday morning when the front desk called Dr. Oliver.

"Mrs. Jones is here to see you."

Dr. Oliver proceeded to walk to the reception area to fetch her patient. Mrs. Jones was dressed in a bright pink top and a purple skirt. She carried a red handbag in her right hand. She wore makeup a bit on the heavy side and very dark sunglasses.

"Good morning Mrs. Jones, it's been a while since I saw you."

Mrs. Jones looked as if she was almost back to her normal self, since leaving the hospital two weeks before.

"I know," replied Mrs. Jones.

She followed Dr. Oliver back to her office.

"Please have a seat. So tell me: how are you doing since you left the hospital?"

"I need to stop taking this horrible medicine or you need to find me another medicine that doesn't make me eat so much."

"I can see you put on few pounds. I'll weigh you at the end. We need to talk about healthy lifestyles and sign you up with the metabolic clinic so we can monitor your weight, sugar and lipids. If things don't go well in the next three months, we can discuss other medication options. This medicine works very well and having an injectable is a great option for patients who don't like or won't take their medicine, such as yourself," explained Dr. Oliver firmly.

She was tired of hearing Mrs. Jones complain about almost any medication that she put her on.

"But the side effects?"

"Remember your discharge plan. You don't want to end up in the hospital again. The judge was very upset that you keep showing up at the emergency room and not taking your medication."

Mrs. Jones seemed to be less argumentative when she heard the consequences of not taking her medication and said, "OK I'll take it for the next three month as you said, but if things don't work out we will have to change it."

"Deal!" said Dr. Oliver who continued to explain the schedule of the injections. "You'll need to come once a month for the shot at the medication clinic. They'll also draw blood for blood work and will check your weight. I'll take you to meet Sarah, the head nurse who runs the medication clinic. By the way are you seeing Eleanor later?"

"Yes, I'm seeing her right after you."

"Great, because we discussed putting in a referral for you at the day program."

"What's that?"

"She'll explain in more detail, but it's a structured activities program that will give you something to do during the day and a chance to meet new people."

"Oh no, I don't want to be with all these crazy people. I'm fine now and I can take care of myself."

"There are different levels of activity and you can be with the high functioning group. Besides, it gives you something to do instead of staying home all day doing nothing," said Dr. Oliver in a hurry and in a way that was non-negotiable. Dr. Oliver was feeling rushed. She already had messages on her phone saying that two patients were waiting for her.

"Ok Mrs. Jones, let us get your weight." She pointed to the scale in her office. "We also need to get your height."

Suddenly Mrs. Jones stopped in the middle of the room as if she had seen a ghost. She took off her glasses, her eyes fixed on the painting that she could now clearly see. Dr. Oliver looked at her in surprise.

"Are you ok? Please, we need to get moving as I have patients waiting. Can you please step on the scale."

Mrs. Jones lifted one foot to step on the scale, but almost fell as she was still looking at the painting. Dr. Oliver supported her to keep her from falling. She pulled the chair closer and helped her to sit down.

"What's happening? Is it this painting?"

"Where did you get this?"

"I just bought it at an auction when I was in Quebec last week. They said it might be a famous artist from Baltimore: Hugh Bolton Jones."

"It is not, it is me Helen Beatrice Jones. I painted this years ago. This is my father and my daughter."

Dr. Oliver couldn't believe her ears. She looked at Mrs. Jones in amazement and then at the signature on the painting - H.B. Jones. N.Y.

"You aren't getting delusional on me are you Mrs. Jones?"

"No, this is the God's honest truth," said Mrs. Jones, who was starting to cry. Dr. Oliver fell back to her seat, and pulled the phone to talk to the front desk.

"Can you please call the therapists of the patients waiting, so they can see them first. I'm going to be here with Mrs. Jones for a while. Something came up."

"Yes doctor," said the receptionist on the other line.

The cell phone rang. It was Bob.

"Hi Honey, anything urgent? I'm very busy," said Dr. Oliver hurriedly.

"Listen, I talked to the curator at the Baltimore Museum of Art. She said she'll be happy to help, but she needs to see the painting. I can swing by your office and pick …'"

"Never mind, I think I've found out who the artist is."

"You did?"

"Yeah, I'll explain later, I have to go."

"Ok bye."

"Mrs. Jones, I am all ears," said Dr. Oliver.

She was bewildered to say the least by all this and could not wait to hear her story. She could feel her heart racing and her breathing was getting tight. She had the feeling that something very important was about to be revealed. She took few deep breaths to calm herself, reminding herself that she was the shrink who was expected to be in control and ready to handle whatever crisis came her way.

6

Helen Beatrice Jones

"I was born Helen Beatrice Jones. I am the youngest of three children, two older boys. We lived in Columbia, South Carolina, a small college town. My Dad was a professor at USC. We had a nice house close to campus. In the summer, we would go to Pawleys Island, a beautiful place near Charleston."

Dr. Oliver interrupted as she was very surprised to hear of her favorite place from one of her patients. "I know Pawleys. I've been there few times. My husband grew up in South Carolina, I love it."

*

Helen was experiencing a flashback of her summer memories there.

"It's almost dinner time. Come clean up. Helen, I need your help setting up the table," her mother, Doris, was calling from the porch of the beautiful beachfront family summer house. Helen was building a sandcastle with her father and two brothers, Jack and Peter, and couldn't hear her mother because of the sound of the crashing waves. Shouting louder and waving her hands, Doris was able to get their attention.

"Let's go guys, we'll finish it after dinner," said Chester to his children.

They were following their father back to the house, with Peter carrying his collection of sand dollars. They all rinsed off with the hose, dried themselves and entered the front porch. On the porch, which was facing the ocean, there was a small dining table with five chairs, two white rocking chairs, and a Pawleys Island hammock hanging from the ceiling. Next to the hammock, hung a wind chime that was gently shaking in the air making a soothing sound. The smell of crab cakes was filling the house.

"Oh yum, crab cakes and corn on the cob, my favorite meal," said Chester, wrapping his arms around his wife who was standing by the stove.

"It's a Father's Day special," said Doris.

"Oh my God, I almost forgot," said Chester.

He looked back at the children in excitement. But they were not there. "Where did they go?" he asked his wife who gave him a look back and shrugged her shoulders as if she did not know.

The children ran upstairs to bring down their surprise Father's Day gifts.

"Oh my God, Doris, this is the best crab cake ever. You should open a restaurant," said Chester to his wife, who smiled back.

"The recipe is in the bank safety deposit box in a sealed envelope with my clear instructions of what to do with it after I'm gone," said Doris.

"Oh I'll be gone long before you, my dear. I hope you reconsider sharing your recipe sooner or even write your own cookbook. These are national treasures, my dear," said Chester.

Doris looked back with a big smile on her face, taking in the compliment, but shaking her head in disagreement to the idea of sharing her recipes. It was time for the gifts and Helen was very excited.

"Me first! Me first!" she said.

She pulled out a portrait of her father that she painted from one of his photos.

"Oh my God baby, you are so talented. I love it … We should send her to art school."

He looked at his wife, who was holding the painting in her hand.

"It is so beautiful Helen, I am getting jealous that I didn't get one for Mother's Day."

"Mom, I thought about it, but I didn't think I could do a better job than the one you have in the living room."

Doris looked a bit nervous.

"Oh sweetie, all that matters is that it's from you. It will be my best one ever."

"Ok mom, I'll try."

Chester got a bit uneasy every time his wife's portrait was talked about. It brought uneasy feelings and memories about his wife and the artist who painted it. All she had told him was that it was done by the German art student who rented a room in their house while going to USC. He could tell however, from the way the portrait was painted, the look in her eyes and the pose, that there was more to it than that.

"Ok Peter, you're next," said Doris sensing the tension in the air. Peter pulled a box from under the dining table and handed it to his father, who got excited again opening the gift.

"Oh Pete you're amazing, where did you find this?" asked Dad, while trying on the Panama straw hat. "It fits perfectly, thanks buddy."

Peter remembered when he was with his father shopping at the golf shop. His dad had tried one on, but they did not have the right size. It was Jack's turn, and he handed a smaller box to his father.

"Jack, how did you buy these buddy?" said Dad, looking at the box of his favorite Cuban cigars.

"I have connections," replied Jack looking at his mom.

Chester got up and gave everyone a kiss and a hug including his wife. "I guess I'm going to try the hat and the cigars tomorrow," he said, referring to a planned golf game with the guys.

"And that is *my* present. You're booked tomorrow at the country club with the guys," said Doris.

"You are an amazing woman," replied Chester, enjoying all the attention he was getting from his family.

"Ready for dessert?" asked Doris.

"Yeah!" everyone yelled at the same time. Doris got up and brought her husband his favorite: key lime pie. The sun was setting, the ocean was getting calm, there was a peaceful relaxing feeling in the air, and the temperature was going down. It was Doris's favorite time of the day for a stroll.

"Who wants to go for a walk?" asked Dad, knowing the answer.

"I'll go," said Doris.

"You guys go," said the kids.

Chester and Doris held hands and went down for a nice stroll. A gust of nice fresh cold air blew over them.

"Did you feel that?"

"What?" replied Chester.

"It's Allison," said Doris.

"You really believe this stuff?"

"You didn't see her? The lady walking down there in the white dress?"

Allison's ghost was one of many famous ghost stories in Pawleys Island; the other famous one was the grey man. Allison, a widow of a fisherman who died at sea, spent years on the look-out waiting for her husband to return. When she died, people believed that her spirit still roamed around the island and she was reported to make appearances on the beach around sunset, when her husband would usually come home from fishing. The grey man on the other hand was believed to be the spirit of one of the original residents of the island who protected and warned the residents of incoming hurricanes. There were many reported sightings of the grey man as well. Rumor had it that those who heeded his warning and left the island kept safe from hurricanes and their homes escaped damage.

"Oh, life was so good back then. I love Pawleys, and boy I always felt very sad when it was time to leave to go back to Columbia to get ready for school," said Mrs. Jones.

Dr. Oliver was totally absorbed in this life story. She could hardly believe that she had had Mrs. Jones for a patient for years and that this was the first time that she was really getting to know her.

"The years went by and life was good, until I was seventeen when I met Mark. We fell in love right away. We spent so much time together. I was very happy, but he had to leave. His family moved to Georgia all of sudden. His father was in the military and it was just one of those things. I was crushed; for weeks I didn't want to get out of bed. I didn't do anything but cry all the time. I was calling him day and night. We went to Pawleys that summer, but I felt horrible. I was so much looking forward to spending the summer with Mark. My Mom tried hard to make me feel better, but nothing helped. That night I decided I was going to end it all. My parents had gone to dinner with friends. I wrote a note to my mother and I went to my Mom's bathroom and took a bunch of Valium pills, I think it was … I remember waking up in the hospital psychiatric ward."

"So this was the first time you saw a psychiatrist?" asked Dr. Oliver.

"Yes. They put me on some kind of amphetamine. It made me really feel good and got me out of the rut. I was able to enjoy life and go back to school after I thought that I was going to drop out. Three months later, they checked me back in the hospital." "What happened?"

"My mom said that I had run away. I took all the cash in the house and my Dad's car. They found me close to Savannah, when the police stopped me. I was doing 90 miles an hour. The car was full of the stuff I bought. According to the officer I was talking non-stop and making no sense, but I don't remember any of this. I guess I was going to see Mark. The doctor said I had a manic episode probably from the speed they put me on."

"So they took you off?" asked Dr. Oliver.

"Yeah, they put me on Lithium and Thorazine. I hated both of them, but my Mom made sure I took them. I remember being on Lithium for years. I was at college at the time."

"What did you study?"

"I was an art major. I loved art. My Dad would always say, 'I have no idea where you got these artistic genes from, neither me nor your mother can draw anything worth a damn'. Mother would always say 'my sister always painted, she was really talented but did not really study'."

Deep inside, Doris was very defensive about her daughter's talents and feeling guilty. Every time the subject of art came up, she would experience a quick flashback of the night Otto painted her portrait. It was that night that she and Otto made love for the first time. There was nobody in the house. Otto wanted to paint her nude, but she refused. He agreed to do a bust instead showing the upper part of her cleavage. The whole painting took less than two hours. It was full of feeling and desire. When he showed her the painting, the desire was so intense that she couldn't resist any more. Helen was conceived that night.

"Don't worry Doris, I'll marry you now if you like," said Otto, after they made love, seeing the nervous look in Doris's eyes.

"Do you love me Otto?" asked Doris.

"I love you even more than I love yellow ochre."

She smiled. Yellow ochre was Otto's favorite color. There was not a single painting that he painted that did not include it. "Yellow ochre is God's gift to me," he had always said.

"I love you too Otto."

She felt less worried. She started to think about how she would tell her parents. But she thought it would not be too much of a surprise, since her parents started to notice something was going on between her and the German art student.

"I noticed you go up a lot to visit with Otto lately," her mother, Beatrice, had said.

"I like art and he thinks I give him good critique of his work."

"Critique, heh?" smiled Beatrice, hugging her daughter. "I just want you to always mind your manners like a good southern girl."

"Not to worry mom, he is always a gentleman."

It was Sunday morning, when the family prepared breakfast before they went to church. Otto always joined them exactly at nine. By ten past nine, he had not shown up.

"You better go call him, the food is getting cold and he is usually on time," said Beatrice.

Doris who ran upstairs to his room. A few seconds later, her parents heard the loudest scream. They ran upstairs to find Doris sitting on the floor sobbing hysterically with her hand over her mouth. In the middle of the room, was Otto hanging from the ceiling. He had hanged himself the night before.

Doris's father climbed up and cut the rope, bringing the body down to the floor. It was devastating for Doris, the shock and the loss was unthinkable. how could he do that to her and why were questions that tormented her for which there were no answers? They had just made love the night before, everything was going great, she was full of hope and happiness and she thought he was too. How could he kill himself? What could have happened in the few hours since she had left him? What if she was pregnant? What would she do?

She started to panic when she missed her next period and was starting to feel nauseous in the mornings. She knew she was pregnant.

"I don't know what to do," said Doris on the phone to her best friend Beverly.

"Meet me at Gatsby's now," said Beverly. "You have two options: get an abortion or marry Chester as soon as possible."

"Are you crazy? Get married now?"

"Didn't he propose to you?"

"Yeah, but I told him I needed time to think."

"Fine. Just tell him 'yes'."

"That isn't fair to Chester."

Doris was always getting marriage proposals from a lot of guys. She was a very beautiful woman, a typical southern beauty, good mannered, and gentle. Her Mom always said, "Doris you will make someone very happy some day, and you will have a beautiful family." Other times she would say, "Doris, you're going to get many marriage proposals, so choose wisely."

Chester came from a good southern family, very well-to-do, a proper and decent gentleman.

"I'll have to tell him," said Doris.

"You will," said Beverly.

"But, ok, let me ask you, how do you think he'll react if you tell him?"

"I think he'll be upset, but he will still want to marry me."

"There you have it!"

"I'm not sure," the confused Doris said.

She knew she needed to make a decision quickly and start the plan of action before her belly start showing. The thought of having an abortion was totally repulsive to her, so that option was out. There was a small chance that Chester might withdraw his marriage offer if he knew she was pregnant, especially if he knew it was Otto. He had never liked him, she could tell from the way he reacted every time he visited or went out with her and Otto was mentioned. She must have subconsciously talked about him a lot, which irritated Chester.

She went to her favorite spot in Columbia: the nearby neighborhood park, her favorite corner was tucked away by the little pond, seeing the ducks and hearing the sound of the small waterfall trickling down the rocks was enough to clear her spirit and her mind. She called it 'the decisions making corner'. This is where she decided to marry Chester.

"Chester do you want to go out for dinner?" she asked.

"Sure Doris, have you thought about ..."

"Yes."

"Does that mean?" said the nervous Chester.

"Can't you wait?" interrupted Doris again. "I've given it a lot of thought and my answer is ... yes!"

Chester yelled.

"Yes!" she said. "Yes!"

He was looking at the other people in the restaurant. He was as happy as could be. Although Doris was looking at Chester, who was holding her hand, her mind was somewhere else. She was checking her own feelings and it felt right. She was happy too and almost guilt free. Her happiness was doubled when she heard Chester say, "I have news for you, we should marry as soon as possible. My father is not doing too well and we are all afraid he might die soon. He told him he wants to see me happily married before it's too late. It is his last wish in this world." Doris couldn't believe her ears. Somehow she knew that God had forgiven her. She looked at him adoringly.

"I totally understand," she said, then paused for a minute, thinking of the long list of tasks that would have to be accomplished and yelled "Oh my God!"

The wedding day was a "miracle" as Beatrice put it. No one thought they could pull it off in three weeks, but they did. A small army of friends and families on both sides helped make it possible. The Chester family home was one of the largest homes in Columbia, South Carolina, with gorgeous magnolias and cypress trees. It was like a scene out of 'Gone with the Wind'.

"I do," said Doris. She still wondered if she had done the right thing, but mostly felt relief. She sneaked a quick glance at her first maid, Beverley, who gave her back a very big approving smile.

"Mrs. Jones, tell me about what happened next?" said Dr. Oliver to her silent and exhausted patient.

"I'm really tired doctor, can we continue later?" replied Helen.

"Tomorrow – I'm going to clear two hours of my schedule. How is that?"

"Ok Doc," replied the tired Helen, who got up, took another look at the painting, and left.

Dr. Oliver was so distracted and preoccupied with what she had heard that she couldn't see any more patients. Mike had peaked in through the peephole in the door many times to make sure she was all right.

"Is everything ok with Mrs. Jones?" he asked.

"Yeah. I just couldn't believe it when she told me she was the one who painted that," she said, pointing to the painting.

"What?" said Mike in amazement.

"I know."

Mike sat down, showing interest in hearing more, but the exhausted Dr. Oliver said, "I'll fill you guys in at our next team meeting. I'm really tired now and I haven't even gotten to the story of the painting with her."

Mike got up.

"Ok, can't wait to hear it," and he left her office.

Dr. Oliver called Rose to ask if she would see her next patient, collected her bags and left. She almost had two accidents driving home because her mind was racing, recollecting every detail over and over again. She did not want to forget anything before she told Bob.

"Hi Honey, so who is the artist?" asked Bob as soon as Melissa arrived home.

"You won't believe this. It's one of my patients!"

"What?"

Bob was setting the table and getting ready to serve dinner.

"It smells good."

Melissa walked towards the oven to see what was for dinner.

"Oh, I made a leg of lamb," said Bob.

"I'm not sure I can eat!"

She sat down at the dinner table, exhaled heavily, and told him about her day. Bob was so intrigued he hardly wanted to touch his food either.

"Did she tell you their names?"

"Who?"

"Her parents."

"No, she just said 'my father and mother' - no names."

"Can you ask her?"

"What are you thinking?"

"I don't know, but there are interesting threads to her story and the research I've been doing on my ..."

"Your mother? Are you saying?"

"I don't know. But South Carolina, Pawleys Island, the visiting artist. I don't know - it could be! My grandmother's told me bits and pieces that are very similar to your patient's story. We need more details to connect the dots, but it could be."

"You mean I might have been treating my mother-in-law all this time?"

That night they stayed up till two o'clock. Melissa tried to remember every detail she had been told and they wrote it down. Bob would get up frequently and pace back and forth. He would compare and double check with his own notebook - where he documented all the research on his missing mother - against what he had heard.

Bob had moved to live with his grandparents when he was seven. His grandmother had told him later that his father and younger sister had died in a car accident. That is all he knew. His mother had disappeared around the same time. Since then, no one knew where she was or whether she was still alive.

7

The College Days

"College was so much fun," said Mrs. Jones to Dr. Oliver when they met the next day.

"First, may I ask you: 'what are your mother's and father's names'?"

"Doris and Chester Ham."

Dr. Oliver almost fell off the edge of her chair, on hearing the names of her husband's grandparents. She was overcome with excitement, fear and confusion all at the same time, but with no time to sort things out and the overwhelming desire to hear more. She decided to control herself from jumping over and hugging her mother-in-law until she heard the rest of the story.

"So you were saying college was a lot of fun?" she asked, with a shaky voice.

"Yes, I loved art. I used to get a thrill, a surge of emotions every time I started a new painting. Thinking about the composition, the colors. When I finally had it all in my head it took me two, maybe three, hours to finish a painting. I'm not saying it was always fun, there were always frustrations when things didn't come out the way I envisaged. I used to give in to my frustrations and give up. Until I met Paul, I would usually either not finish what I started, or destroy the canvas, mix all the colors together, or wipe it off."

"Who's Paul?" asked Dr. Oliver, who was intensely concentrating on every word that had came out of her patient's mouth. The only other time she felt that way was during her board examination, where she wanted to make sure she didn't miss any detail and asked the right questions. She wrote down every word. She wanted to have everything documented and not leave any details to memory for the debriefing with Bob later.

"Paul was my art teacher. Having watched me destroy many of my projects, he said, 'You really have to get beyond this phase, otherwise you'll never finish a painting. Even the masters get to a point where they hate their work. Imagine if they did what you did. We wouldn't have any of these masterpieces to enjoy. Move away, leave it alone for a while, calm yourself down, come back to it later – you'll be amazed what you can do to turn it around, and boy when it is finished will you be happy you stuck with it.' It worked, I was much more in touch with my emotions and controlling my anger," said Mrs. Jones, pointing to the painting. "This is my father and my daughter. When she was six months old, my father came to visit. It was Christmas. Maybe it was the only, time he visited me. I remember it was a very cold night. He had Sophie in his lap and was tickling her, but she didn't like it and was crying. It was adorable - I sketched it for later. The light was perfect." She paused. She was getting teary-eyed remembering these precious moments and imaging how old her daughter would have been had she lived, what would be she doing, if she would be married and what her grandchildren might look like.

"It is so precious," said Dr. Oliver as she handed her patient the box of tissues on her desk. "How did it end up in Canada?"

She immediately regretted asking the question. She did not want to rush events or make Mrs. Jones forget what she was about to say.

"I don't really know. I had it hanging in our home for years. How it ended up there, I have no idea."

"I'm going to ask the Gallery if they have any records from the previous owner and I'll definitely let you know." Dr. Oliver quickly redirected the conversation to keep things on track. "Tell me about college." Helen paused for a while as if she was having a flashback.

*

Helen was known in college as flamboyant, promiscuous and seductive. There were always rumors surrounding her and stories about her sleeping with half the men on campus - students and faculty, without restraint. Helen definitely gave a lot of ammunition for the rumors. One day, a model did not show up for the scheduled class.

"Sorry guys, but the model just called in sick. We can either do another still life or ... " said Paul.

But before he finished his sentence Helen had raised her hand.

"I volunteer!"

Paul was not expecting that forward suggestion from one of his students, especially the one he was having feelings for. All the guys in the class were cheering.

"Helen! Helen!"

After few seconds of hesitation, Paul thought it wouldn't be a bad idea to have a chance to see that gorgeous sexy body anyway.

"Ok, but we can't pay you."

"No problem. I'll make the sacrifice for the sake of art," Helen replied seductively.

The other girls in the class were looking at each other as if to affirm their opinion of her as a slut. Helen moved to the front and started taking off her clothes while looking at the guys in the room, who all tried to pretend to behave professionally. Paul was having second thoughts and wondered if he was breaking any of the school rules. But before he could open his mouth, it was too late: Helen was naked in front of the class.

Some of the best nude art was produced in the class that day. Paul walked around watching the students paint and critiquing their work. "Wow! I'm really pleased by how many good pieces are shaping up," he said, giving each student suggestions about the shape of the breasts or the color of the eyes.

"Pathetic!" Paul was commenting on one painting of a very small figure, almost a couple of inches long, with very obscure features, that one of the girls was working on. She looked back at the teacher and shrugged her shoulders.

"This is how I feel," she said.

Helen could care less what the others thought of her. However, after two abortions in one year, and only having friends that were boys, Doris suggested taking her daughter to see another psychiatrist.

"I don't want to see a shrink. There's nothing wrong with me, Mother. Just leave me alone!" Helen protested.

"I've had it with you young lady. Either you go see a psychiatrist or you leave this house!" said her exhausted mother.

"Ok bye," said Helen on her way out, slamming the door behind her.

Doris was not sure if she had let her anger take over and was worried where her daughter might go or end up. She was having visions of Helen prostituting herself, getting into drugs and ending up dying on the street. She ran after her daughter.

"Helen, please listen to me."

Helen was far ahead on her way to her thinking corner. Doris ran to the house to get her car keys and drove to chase her daughter. She knew where to find her.

Helen got up and started to walk away when she saw her mother coming towards her, but Doris quickened her pace.

"Helen please wait. I'm sorry, I didn't mean what I said. I just want to help you and I don't know how."

Helen stopped and looked at her mother.

"No shrinks!"

"Ok," said Doris. "Baby, I want the best for you. I want you to be happy. I feel very helpless seeing you go through this and not being able to do anything."

"I feel fine, mother. There's nothing wrong with me, I'm very happy."

"But baby, I can see it. I'm living it with you. Your moods change all the time. This is not normal. This is a small town. You don't think I hear the rumors about you? You remind me of your fath ... " Doris stopped suddenly and did not finish her sentence.

"My father? What about him? He's the most level-headed person I know."

Doris was not about to reveal to her daughter who her biological father was, at least not now. She ignored her daughter's question.

"Remember what the doctors say about bipolar illness."

"I don't have bipolar."

"But you had …" interrupted Helen.

"That was from the speed they gave me when I was depressed."

"You stopped your Lithium which was really helping. I could see a difference," said Doris.

"I couldn't."

"Can we just please try it again for a short period? Please, just for me," pleaded Doris.

Helen was softening up a bit. Deep inside, she had a feeling that something strange was going on with her.

"Ok, I'll try it again for three months just to prove to you that it's not going to make any difference."

"I'll give it to you like before," said Doris.

"Fine!"

They kept walking. Doris, wrapped her right arm around her daughter's waist and gave her a kiss on the top of her head.

"Thank you my dearest daughter. So you have met many boyfriends: any of them serious?"

"You mean you want me to get married?"

"That will be the happiest day of my life. I'll make you a wedding the state of South Carolina will talk about for years to come."

Helen felt safe, happy and very special. She started daydreaming, seeing herself in a wedding gown. Standing next to her, were many potential husbands. However, of the numerous guys she had dated none of them felt like the right one.

"Helen, you want to go for dinner?" Paul asked.

Helen who was alone in the studio putting some final touches on a painting. "I thought there were rules against that kind of thing?" she answered.

"What kind of a thing?" asked Paul, pretending he did not understand.

"Teacher-student dating thing."

"I think there may be, but I don't frankly care."

"Weren't you reprimanded by the Dean for letting me pose in front of the class?" said Helen, trying to put some sense in his head.

"You heard, heh?"

"Everyone heard! You don't really care much about rules do you Professor?" Helen had a wicked smile on her face.

"I guess you could say that."

Helen remembered the reason she liked Paul and felt connected to him. "So what exactly do you like about me, Professor? My personality or my body?" she asked in a sneaky way.

"Let us say both."

"When and where?" asked Helen, speeding up the conversation as the sound of approaching footsteps were heard.

"Tomorrow night at Joe's," said Paul.

"Good night professor," said the cleaning person, who had arrived to tidy up the studio.

Paul pretended he was engrossed in Helen's painting. He let a few seconds go by before he replied, "Oh, good night

George". He then proceeded to give feedback to Helen. "It looks much better. I like what you did with the background, it makes the flowers really stand out, good job," and proceeded to walk away.

Joe's was a noisy and dark nightclub, not very popular with the younger crowd. The place was particularly crowded that night. The club was hosting Edgar Paws: a famous blues musician from Mississippi who was performing in South Carolina for the first time. Paul loved blues and he was looking forward to the evening. With the anticipated excitement of going on a date with Helen, having a Scotch and smoking a cigar, he was feeling almost high.

Paul sat on a corner table sketching the scene in his sketchpad which he always carried with him. The dim blue and yellow lights mixed in a nice green tone, the smoke rising up in the room giving it a foggy eerie sensation. Edgar and the accompanying musicians were already on the stage tuning their instruments.

It was already ten past eight, but he knew she was never on time, even for the class. At eight thirty, he was feeling a bit of disappointment that she might not actually show up. It did not occur to him that he might be stood up by one of his students. He thought of how complicated things might get at the class if she did not show up. He was getting a bit paranoid remembering what she said about the rules. Maybe he did not really understood her at all, maybe he had the wrong impression of her altogether. As he was going through these emotions, she showed up at the door. He immediately felt relief. He waved his hand, so she could see where he was sitting.

"Sorry I'm late. I got lost trying to find the place."

"Don't worry about it, I'm glad you're here," continued Paul. "You're in for a treat tonight, one of the best blues musicians on the east coast is performing."

"Oh, I like blues - but after the third song it all feels the same to me."

"That's not unusual. You just have to focus on the story."

"Ok, I'll give it a try."

He ordered the oysters and she ordered the catfish. Edgar started singing, "I was born the day of the eclipse and my baby was named after a hurricane." Helen was following Paul's advice and was focusing on the story. That line certainly grabbed her attention. They were both totally absorbed in the ambiance, the food and the loud music. They looked at each other, but did not speak. He held her hand. She let him and gave him a big smile and said, "I'm happy."

"Me too," said Paul.

Helen went to Paul's place that night. He invited her and she agreed. His apartment was a big studio with a bed at the corner, no place to sit to have a conversation. He had his easel in the middle of the room. On it was an unfinished canvas of a nude body.

"Is that me?" asked Helen.

"Yep."

"Do you want to finish it?"

"Sure," he said.

She took off her clothes and sat on the bar stool, her arms behind her and her head tilted slightly backward. He grabbed his brush and his palate and turned on his favorite jazz tape. She was so irresistible, he had an erection. But he wanted to finish the painting first; he wanted his feelings and intense desire for her to come out in the painting. By the time the tape was almost over, he was done. It was an exquisite painting full of desire and emotion. He took off his clothes and they made passionate love. She whispered in his ear, "I don't have protection," but that did not make any difference.

*

"Mom, I think I'm pregnant," Helen said to her mother few weeks later, after the night with Paul.

"Not again!" yelled her mother who was looking forward to an uneventful Sunday. "Are you taking your Lithium?"

"You are giving it to me."

"You're not supposed to get pregnant while you're taking it."

"Well I wasn't planning on it, it just happened."

"Pregnancy doesn't just *happen*, Helen," said her angry mother.

"I'm going to get an abortion."

"Who is the father?"

"You don't know him."

Helen was trying to protect Paul in case there were some ramifications with him being her teacher.

"I need to get ready to go to church, are you coming?" asked Doris who needed time out to think.

"No, I'm very tired today. I think I'm going to rest at home."

After her mother left the house, Helen called Paul.

"I'm pregnant."

"Meet me in half an hour," said Paul.

They met for coffee at the nearby café.

"Let's get married," said Paul.

"Would you have married me if I wasn't pregnant?"

"I would, I was going to ask you to marry me the next time we met. I love you Helen, all of you, not just your body. We have so much in common. I got a job offer at NYU and I think I'm going to take it."

"When?"

"January."

"I have bipolar disorder and I am on Lithium," said Helen, as if in a confession. "I feel normal most of the time, but at times I get moody and maybe you will hate me then."

"I want to know all about it, but nothing will change my feelings about you."

"I love you."

"Ok, ask me," said Helen.

"Ask you what?"

"To marry me."

Paul kneeled in front of her. "Helen, I love you so much and I want to spend the rest of my life with you, would you marry me?"

"Yes," she said.

They walked home. Her parents had just arrived back from church.

"Dad, Mom, this is Paul. He just asked me to marry him and I accepted," said Helen.

The surprised parents looked at each other with their mouths wide open.

"Oh, nice to meet you Paul," said Chester.

"Honey, why don't you and Paul get to know each other while I make some iced tea," said Doris while grabbing her daughter's arm and guiding her to the kitchen. Doris thought how ironic it was that her daughter was going through almost the same emotional rollercoaster ride that she went through in falling in love with Otto and getting pregnant. She wanted to be supportive of her daughter, not judgmental. She wanted to be protective of her daughter but at the same time she wanted her to be happy. Deep inside, she was scared that Helen would not have a normal life like most young women – with a husband and a family. Meeting Paul, although not in the perfect circumstances that she would have wanted, was still a very good thing as far as giving her hope that Helen could have a family. The idea that in less than nine months she could be holding her grandchild sent a warm thrill to her heart. She collected her thoughts and let a big sigh.

"So is he the father?"

"Yes."

"He seems to be a nice guy, do you love him?"

"Very much."

"Does he know about ..."

"I told him and it is ok." Helen could tell her mother was referring to her mental illness. They hugged.

"I want the best for you," said Doris.

"I know Mom. He's really a good guy and we have so much in common."

Doris was not sure how to respond to that last bit of information. All she knew was she had that uneasy feeling up her spine. They went back to the porch where Chester and Paul were sitting. The two of them were smoking cigars.

"Honey, I guess it is déjà vu all over again," said Chester. Doris looked at him puzzled. "We have to arrange another wedding in three weeks. Mr. Artist here has to leave his position at USC, go back to New Jersey to settle some family matter, and get ready to move to New York ... and somewhere in there, get married and have a honeymoon - all this in three weeks."

Doris smiled. "I think I'm going to open a speedy wedding planner business."

They all laughed.

"We are keeping the baby," said Helen to her mother after her father left.

"You are? Do you understand the problem with the Lithium?"

"We do. We talked to the doctor and we read about it and we're willing to take the risk. Meanwhile I'm stopping it."

8

The Joneses

The wedding was simple but elegant: immediate family and close friends only. Helen did not have too many close girlfriends who were willing or could come to the wedding. She did however have many friends who were boys. So on her wedding day, at her request, three of them dressed as girls and pretended to be the bridesmaids. Her father kept asking who these girls were. Her mother said, "These are her friends from way back when. Friends she has kept in touch with. You don't know them because you were never involved in your kids' lives." Chester definitely did not want to have this conversation on his daughter's wedding day, so he walked away.

The couple took off to Pawleys Island for a short honeymoon. Helen was not feeling good. The wedding, the pregnancy, and the anticipated move, were all taking their toll.

"I don't want to get up. Leave me please. I want to sleep some more," she said, the morning after her wedding when Paul tried to wake her.

So he made some coffee and went for a walk on the beach. He came back, but she was still asleep.

"Honey do you want some breakfast?"

She waved her hand for him to go away and went back to sleep. He left her alone and went to the kitchen, made some breakfast and read the paper.

He was not planning on spending the first day of his honeymoon alone and he did not know what to do. He went back and forth a few times checking on his wife, but she was sound asleep. He wrote a note for her saying he was going for a walk to explore the shops down town. He spent most of the day looking at the shops and the galleries, bought some flowers, then decided to go back to see if Helen was up. She was sitting in bed crying profusely.

"Honey, what's wrong?"

"I feel horrible, I don't want to get out of bed."

"That's ok baby, you've been through a lot the last few weeks. I'm pretty stressed out myself. But maybe going out to get some fresh air and have a nice dinner will do you good?"

"I'm sorry honey, but I don't feel like being around people right now and I'm not really hungry."

The phone rang. "Hi Doris, we're ok. Though Helen isn't feeling good. The pregnancy and the stress, you know," said Paul.

"She may be getting depressed. Please watch her and if she doesn't get better, we should call Dr. Wanamaker."

"Will do."

Helen ran to the bathroom to throw up, then crawled back in bed. Paul covered her and dimmed the light, went out to the living room and turned on the TV.

The night was rough with Helen tossing and turning all night, mumbling words in her sleep. Paul did not get any deep sleep that night either. He felt very exhausted the next day.

Helen got up and ran to the bathroom again to throw up, waking Paul. She came back to bed, pulled the covers over her, and said, "If you want a divorce I'll understand."

He turned towards her and hugged her. "I'm not a quitter. I'm in it for the long haul, love you."

She kissed his hand and went back to sleep.

*

"My wife doesn't want to get out of bed, she's crying all the time and throwing up. She hasn't had anything to eat for three days now," Paul said to Dr. Wanamaker.

"Can you come to see me? I'm in the Charleston office on Thursdays and Fridays which is very close to Pawleys."

"How have you been feeling Helen?" asked Dr. Wanamaker.

"Miserable" answered Helen.

"Doc, I caught her last night as she was about to slash her wrist with my shaving razor."

"Is that true?"

"I can't take this anymore."

"We'll have to put you back on Lithium and maybe an anti-depressant as well. I'd like to admit you to the hospital for few days until the medicine takes hold so we can watch you to make sure you and the baby are ok."

She looked at her husband as if asking him what he thought. He was nodding his head, approving of the plan.

"I think it's a good idea."

"What about the baby with all these medications?"

"We just have to watch things and hope for the best. But you do need to be back on the medicine."

She was admitted to the psychiatry ward, put on suicide watch, and was back on medications. The OB consultant came to check on her.

"Everything seems to be ok. I'll recommend something for the morning sickness. Do check back with me at the clinic when you leave."

By the fourth day, things were getting better: the fluids and the nutrition helped, the morning sickness was subsiding. Paul, who practically spent the honeymoon in the hospital with his wife, had gone to get coffee from the hospital cafeteria when Doris walked in.

"How's my girl?" she asked, opening the curtains and putting a bunch of flowers in the pot.

"Much better. I'm sorry Mom."

Doris gave her a big hug and a kiss.

"The doctors are saying everything is stable and the baby is growing well, thank God."

"Have you guys been thinking of names for the baby?"

"Robert Chester Jones if it's a boy and Doris Ann Jones if it's a girl." Helen looked at her mother appreciatively.

"Oh sweetie, don't you want to name her one of those new modern names?"

"No, Doris is it," insisted Helen.

Paul walked back in.

"Oh, hi Doris, do you see how much better she's getting?" he said, while hugging his wife.

"I know, touch wood. She is doing a lot better."

"Did the doctors say anything about when she might leave? Hopefully you can spend a couple of days relaxing before you have to leave."

"No they haven't, but maybe today they'll tell us."

"Can I leave today please doctor?" asked Helen of Dr. Wanamaker, when he came to check on her.

"Well, I think you're doing a lot better and I don't see why we need to keep you here much longer. A couple of days on the beach will do you more good than being here."

"Oh thanks Doctor."

"I want to see you a week from now in the clinic. We'll have the nurse in charge make the appointment for you. Any questions?"

"No, I'm all clear."

"Oh, it's so good to be home," said Helen while opening the window and getting a deep breath of fresh air.

"Welcome home, baby," said Paul.

Doris went back to Columbia to let the newlyweds enjoy some time alone.

"I'm famished, what smells so good?"

Paul had gone earlier to the fresh seafood market and loaded on crab meat and oysters.

"Crab cakes and oysters Rockefeller."

"Really?" Helen looked impressed.

"It's your mother's special recipe too."

"No! She gave you the recipe?" said Helen in disbelief.

"Are you kidding? She prepared everything before she left and just left me instructions on how to warm it."

They had two good days at last. Helen was getting her spirits back and they talked about the future and the baby. Paul had to go to New Jersey for few days, then to New York to sign the contract for the new position and to look for a place to live. Driving north, Paul had a lot of time to think and reflect on what he had gotten himself into, marrying a bipolar. He had no idea what he had let himself in for or how bad it could get. Thank God he was not working and Helen's mother was nearby. But 'what if?' he thought to himself, 'Just have to take it one day at a time. She needs to be on her medications, no questions about it. And New York is not that far.' He was trying to reassure himself for now. But deep inside, he was having a tinge of uneasiness and an unsettling feeling. He thought of the baby and the chance of her being born with some defects from Lithium or the chance of growing up like her mother. 'Thank God, I'm not a worrier,' he thought to himself, 'otherwise I'd be worrying all the time: short-term worry; long-term worry; and lifelong permanent worry. I could go crazy.' Then, as he always did to get out of that gloom, he resigned himself to the fact that there was nothing much he could do about it, but leave it to the powers that be. Let the chips fall where they may.

Helen went back to Columbia to rest and regain her full strength before the move. She was as sweet as could be.

"Being a mom is doing something to you, I think. I'm seeing a side of you that I haven't seen before," said Doris.

"I'm very happy mom. I'm just praying the baby will be ok with all these medications I'm taking," replied Helen.

"He will. I know it."

"How do you know it's a 'he'?" asked Helen.

"I can tell from the shape of your tummy and I can see few hairs on your upper lip."

Helen panicked and covered her upper lip. "You mean I'm growing a moustache?"

"Sort of. They say when you're carrying a boy you get some testosterone in your system."

"Oh boy, no wonder I'm feeling very horny lately."

"That too. I remembered when I was pregnant with your brothers, I was very horny too. I wanted to have sex all the time. Your poor Dad was so scared to have sex with me. He thought it might harm the baby."

"Does it?"

"The doctor said there was no problem."

"So it is Bobby then?" Helen said.

"I think so."

Bobby was born a healthy seven pounds baby, a little sluggish at birth, but nothing was wrong with him physically. The whole family was there.

*

"I wanted my children to be born in South Carolina. I didn't want them to be Yankees," said Helen to Dr. Oliver who was in tears and shock, not believing that she was hearing about the birth of her husband. The whole thing was too much to take, even for a psychiatrist who was well trained in how to control her emotions.

"Dr. Oliver, why are you crying?"

"I'll tell you later. But tell more about life in New York and the new baby."

Dr. Oliver looked down at her notebook and dried her nose with a tissue paper.

"New York was hectic. I never really liked it, too fast paced for me. But the art scene was amazing. Every weekend we would go to a new exhibition. Paul loved it; it was very stimulating for him. He exhibited a few times. He made good money selling some of his work besides teaching. Our apartment was not big, but we made sure there was a studio for both of us. I painted too, mostly portraits of family, the children." Helen looked over at the painting in the office as if to say, 'Just like that one'.

"Oh, so you had other children?" interrupted Dr. Oliver intrigued by the chance to find out about other family members. Helen was quiet, her eyes were getting wet. Then she started to talk.

"Sophie was born two years after Bobby. Unfortunately she had some heart problems. The doctor said it was the Lithium, which I couldn't stop. I wish I had though. She was fragile and cute as could be. Paul adored her, she was the love of his life. He was so protective of her. She couldn't do a lot of the physical stuff or run around like other kids do. She would always run out of breath. He was always there to help her and encourage her."

She looked at the painting again. Dr. Oliver turned to look too and said, "Oh, she is adorable."

"Was," said Helen.

"Oh, I'm so sorry. What happened - her heart troubles?"

"No." Helen was crying and drying her tears. She looked spacey as if she was having another flashback. "It was a rainy Friday night. We were getting ready to go to a reception for a new Japanese artist who was exhibiting in Soho …"

"Honey what is taking so long? We need to go!" said Paul, hurrying his wife who was upstairs getting ready. Helen walked downstairs dressed in a brightly colored kimono, her face painted white and her hair jet black. She was holding baby Sophie in her arms. The baby was also dressed in a baby kimono with the same makeup and hairdo.

"Tata!" said Helen raising her left arm. Paul was trying not to laugh.

"What are you doing Helen? You can't go out like this. This is a reception not a Halloween party."

"But it is Japanese artist, right? I just wanted to blend in, make the guy feel at home. They will have sushi right? Better have Unagi, my favorite. Do you think they will have Unagi? Should we call them to make sure?" Helen was rambling non-stop.

"Shit Helen, did you stop your medicine again? Fuck! I've had it with you!" Paul was furious.

"I don't need the God damn medicine! There's nothing wrong with me!" yelled Helen. She started to cry. Her makeup was melting over her face, which made her look really crazy.

"Go look at your face. You look nuts. You *are* nuts. I'm done. I'm leaving. We're both leaving!" He grabbed the baby from her arms, ran outside, put her in the back car seat and drove off like a bat out of hell. He was trying to make it to the opening on time. He was set to introduce the artist, so the show could not start without him. On the way, he needed to swing over the babysitter's house to drop off the baby. Looking over his watch constantly, he yelled at the red traffic lights and the other drivers who refused to give him way. He swerved the car sharply, trying to go around traffic, crossing into the lane of the incoming traffic, losing control in the wet weather and smashing the car head on into a delivery truck, going under it. The car was a piece of twisted metal by the time police arrived.

"I got a call from the police. Paul died on the spot and Sophie died in the hospital. According to the police report, he had a head-on collision trying to go around the traffic," said Helen.

"I'm so sorry. What about your son?" asked a teary-eyed Dr. Oliver.

"Bobby was at a sleepover at his friend's house that night. I remember leaving the house to go to the hospital, but I never made it there. All I remember is that I hitchhiked on the highway and I remember getting in a truck."

9

Running Away

"Do you speak English?" the truck driver had asked the lady in the Kimono.

"Yes, where you heading?"

"Richmond, Virginia."

"Can you drop me off in South Carolina on the way?"

"Did you hear me lady? I'm only going to Richmond. I can take you there. Then you have to figure out how to go to South Carolina from there."

"Ok," she said.

"Hop in," said the driver, looking at her clothes. "Are you going to a party or something?"

"Yeah, it's a funeral party for a Japanese friend. They asked everyone to dress appropriately so the spirit of the dead person thinks he's in Japan. They couldn't afford doing the funeral in Japan and they don't want his spirit to be stuck in South Carolina. It's a Japanese spiritual thing. Do you like sushi? I like Unagi. It is eel. Maybe we should go to Japan, do you know the way? Just drive to Alaska, then cross to Russia, and down to Japan. I did it before. It's about twenty hours' drive, but if you step on it we can be there in ten."

She was looking at the driver, who had his mouth half-open. He was looking at her out of the corner of his eye, while trying to keep his focus on the road.

"Sure I'll go. I just need to gas-up the truck," said the driver, as he pulled into the gas station. Realizing he had picked up a nutcase, his mind was made up to get rid of her. "I need to stop for a coffee and go to the boys' room. Let's go inside. Just go in and wait for me in the restaurant and I'll be right there." After Helen went in, he immediately turned around, got in his truck and drove away.

Helen found herself alone in the restaurant. It did not take a second for people walking by to realize they are looking at a crazy person. Her hair was wet and the black dye was all over her face - her makeup running from standing in the rain, hitchhiking. She looked like a Dalmatian with white and black spots all over her face. Her Kimono was getting unraveled, with her thighs showing and her left breast sticking out.

"Can I help you Madam?" said the receptionist at the restaurant.

"Yeah I am here with a friend. Do you have sushi?"

"No Madam we don't."

Helen walked away looking confused, and headed to the men's room to try to find the truck driver. She was getting more agitated by then, looking at the guys at the urinals trying to find him. The guys were shocked seeing a half-naked woman walking around looking at them. They interrupted their act as they tried to hide their private parts. When she did not see the driver, she started knocking on the closed doors of the stalls.

"Hey you! Mr. Truck Driver, whatever your name is, they don't have sushi. Let's go somewhere else."

The security guys soon walked in. "Madam you can't be here". They pulled her out and into a private office nearby.

"Madam do you have an ID?" asked one of the security officers.

"No, but everyone knows me. I am Kiko the famous Japanese singer. I need to go to South Carolina, I have a performance tonight. Call a cab. Do you know Dominigo? Call Dominigo. Tell him Kiko is here. Tell him to bring sushi."

"Ok Ms. Kiko, we'll have to admit you for the night," said the doctor on call at the New Jersey State hospital. She was given a Haldol injection, which knocked her out for the night.

*

"I don't know where my daughter is," said Doris to the hospital attendant when she arrived in New York, after hearing the tragic news.

"We didn't hear from her either," said the friend who had been taking care of Bobby and who had accompanied Doris to the hospital.

The funeral was held in Trenton, New Jersey. Paul was originally from a few blocks away from the state hospital where Helen was. Doris filed court papers to take custody of Bobby, since his mother was missing. At the same time, she filed papers to declare her daughter incompetent in absentia, to be able to dispose of the house and other belongings. After the garage sale, Doris drove home to South Carolina with Bobby. Besides Bobby's clothes and toys, the only other items she brought home were Paul and Helen's paintings, except for the one that ended up in Quebec, somehow by mistake it was sold in the garage sale

"Doctor, we don't know where she is," said the day nurse when Helen was discovered missing at the state hospital. She had snuck out of the unit in the early morning hours, while breakfast was being brought in. Still groggy from the Haldol, she dragged herself to the nearby 7-Eleven, poured herself a cup of coffee, and walked away.

"Hi, my name is Kiko," she said to a group of homeless men who were living under a highway overpass. They were very dirty, smelly and disheveled; each had their own cardboard box and a shopping cart loaded with stuffed trash bags. They looked at her and did not say a word.

Helen was not sure what to expect, what she was doing, or where she was going. All she was sure about was that she was not going to stay in a state hospital. She needed time to think, but her thinking was not clear. Her mind was racing, everything was confused and meshed together. She constantly got images of her family, the truck ride, and her mother - but she could not remember why she had left or where she was heading.

She was talking to herself all the time, while looking at the other guys who were also talking to themselves. Even though they were living in close proximity to one another, each was totally absorbed in their own world. They hardly interacted with each other. The main reason they were together was because they figured that this spot was a safe hideaway from police and the rain. Many police cars drove by, but they didn't bother them unless they did something to disturb the peace or if the weather was too cold to be outside. Helen would get up and pace for few steps as if she was going to walk away, but ended up coming back to the same spot. She was getting hungry, so she walked to the street corner nearby, towards the trash cans to look for something to eat.

"There's a soup kitchen on Elm Street just few blocks from here," said a woman who was walking by. Helen looked at her strangely. The woman started to give her directions on how to get there.

"Do they have sushi?."

"I don't think so, but you never know," said the woman with a smile. "You know what, I'm actually headed in the same direction. I can show you the way if you want." She was sure that Helen wouldn't be able to find the place on her own.

Helen mumbled something in return and the two women started walking together.

"I take it you aren't from around here?"

"I'm from Japan. My name is Kiko, what's yours?" asked Helen

"My name is Claire. So is this your first visit to the United States?"

"Yes, I'm going to South Carolina. My driver's gone to pee and then he'll come to pick me up. You can come with us." Helen was looking suspiciously at the people walking by, while continuing to mumble to herself.

"Thank you. What are you going to do in South Carolina?" asked Claire.

"Sing concerts, Japanese opera."

"What's it about?"

"About a woman, husband dies, Sophie, Sophie ... " Helen paused briefly, as if her brain was trying to connect the dots. But she got distracted again by the long line-up at the soup kitchen.

"We're here," said Claire, who was getting ready to leave. "Good luck with the concert."

"You're coming right? Front seat, just ask for Kiko."

"Thanks again. I'll try," answered Claire and waved goodbye.

Helen was very hungry and was feeling very special, so she walked to the front of the line.

"Hey, the line starts here, it ends there!" said the angry man at the front, pointing to the end of the line.

"Shut up you idiot! Bodyguard, take this man to jail now! I am Kiko!" said Helen to the man who was in line behind the angry man. She started singing out loud to the crowd. Some were cheering her and others were angrily shouting.

"Shut up! Go back to the end of the line!"

Suddenly, a man appeared from the crowd and pulled her away.

"They're going to call the police and they'll put you back in the hospital. Come with me."

Helen looked at the strange man and decided to go with him.

"I'm Jack. I'm bipolar, schizophrenic and schizoaffective. The doctors can't seem to make up their minds."

"I am Kiko. I am normal."

"You have a nice voice. I play the piano. Maybe you and I could be a team? Come, let us go to another soup kitchen. It's only fifteen minutes away. I'm visiting my sister, but the food at the soup kitchen is better."

"Where are you from?"

"South Japan," answered Helen. "I need to go to South Carolina."

"I'm from Virginia. You can come with me, the same bus goes to South Carolina. I leave in two days. Where are you staying?"

"I'm waiting for my driver to pick me up."

"You can stay with me. My sister won't mind."

*

"Hi Jack, what took you so long? The food is cold by now, do you want me to heat it up?" said Ann, Jack's sister.

"We ate already."

"You went to the soup kitchen again? I made you meatloaf. Who is this?" Ann was looking at Helen.

"This is Kiko. She's normal. We met at the ... movies."

"Oh, you went to the movies."

"Yes, Kiko is going to South Carolina, so she'll leave with me on the bus. Can she stay for a couple of days?" Jack's voice was choking up a bit because he was not sure what his sister would say.

"Sure, Buddy. Just keep it quiet up there," answered Ann with a wicked smile.

Ann loved her older brother dearly and always wished for him a normal life. Seeing him walking in with a woman reminded her of her teenage son introducing his first girlfriend. Jack gave Helen an encouraging sure look, as if to say 'Didn't I tell you everything will be ok?' and invited her in.

"Hungry?" he asked.

"Yes," answered Helen, who did not get enough to eat at the soup kitchen. They sat down to eat. Ann heated the food again and attempted to sit down with them, but decided not to.

"Oh this meatloaf is delicious," said Helen while chewing on a bit. Ann, who waited in the kitchen where she could hear what they were saying, smiled. She wanted to know more about the stranger her brother had brought to her house.

They looked very cute together. Helen was eating while Jack was watching.

"I used to think there was nothing wrong with me," Jack started saying, "but all the doctors and therapists kept telling me that I have a disease - a chemical imbalance - so I take medicine."

He showed her the pills he was supposed to take at bedtime.

"You don't need medicine."

Ann, listening in the kitchen did not like that comment. She showed up quickly with pumpkin pie.

"Pie anyone?"

She gave Helen a sharp look and said to her brother, "Jack don't forget to take your medicine."

Jack, who knew that taking his medication was a precondition for his staying in the house, popped the pills into his mouth and drank a glass of water. Ann then looked at Helen, offering to refill her glass of water.

"Kiko, do you need to take your medicine?"

"I don't take medicine. I don't need medicine – there's nothing wrong with me."

"Well Jack does and he's really doing great since he decided he needed to take his medicine all the time, right Jack?"

"Yep," answered her brother. "We're going to go upstairs now."

Jack was trying to keep things from escalating. He was getting fond of Helen and wanted to avoid any chance his sister might kick her out of the house.

"Ok good night. Again, be quiet. The kids' bedroom is right across from you."

"We will," said Jack.

Helen couldn't sleep, She was pacing all night. Jack was worried his sister would hear the footsteps. She did hear them. Ann knocked on the door of their room.

"Is everything ok in there? Can you stop pacing? I can't sleep. I have to go to work bright and early."

Jack offered Helen a pill.

"Here Kiko."

"I don't need medicine," she said.

"It will help you sleep, trust me."

She took it and crawled in bed next to him. Helen slept the whole two days she stayed there.

"Wake up sleepy head, we have to get ready to leave," said Jack, trying to wake Helen up on the third day. Helen woke up tired and groggy. "You slept for two days," said Jack.

After breakfast, they walked to the Greyhound bus station. He paid for her ticket to Columbia, South Carolina.

"Do you want another pill?" asked Jack.

She opened her hand and took it. She went back to sleep throughout the ten-hour drive to Virginia. When they got close to the state border, Jack tried to wake her up so he could say goodbye.

"Where are we?" she asked, with eyes half open.

"We just crossed the Virginia border. My stop is coming up next." He got up to get his bag and sat down waiting for the bus to stop.

"Kiko, what is your address so I can come and visit you?"

"I am going with you."

"Are you sure?" asked Jack, who had been wishing that she would do exactly that.

Helen's mania was quieting down; the sleep she got and the medication helped. She started to feel that something horrible had happened, she couldn't remember the details, but it was a gut feeling and she did not want to face it or know what it was. All she knew was that she had this overwhelming feeling that she wanted to flee from and escape. Going to Columbia, South Carolina, was out of the question at this time.

"Next stop, Mount Vernon, Virginia," said the bus driver.

They both got up and left.

"Welcome to my home" said Jack "You can stay here as much as you like."

"Where's the bedroom?" asked Helen, who crawled into bed and went back to sleep.

*

Doris called all hospitals and police departments in New York with no luck. She wrote to Paul's family, friends and staff at NYU to see if anyone had any news about where her daughter might be. With no leads, she finally gave up searching. Chester's health was deteriorating with late stage colon cancer and he died three months later. The boys both moved away with their families. She was left all alone, tired and sad. At fifty-three she looked like she was in her seventies.

"It's only you and me now. We'll have to take care of each other," said Doris to Bobby, who was sitting on her lap. A tear rolled down her cheek.

"I'll take care of you grandma. I know how to make pancakes," said Bobby wiping her tear away. Doris laughed and gave him a big kiss.

*

A week after she arrived at Virginia, she remembered what had happened. She remembered that she was supposed to go to the county hospital in New York to identify the bodies of her husband and her daughter. She remembered little Bobby whom she left with the neighbors. She remembered her mother. All this was overwhelming.

Helen went into a very severe depression and decided she needed to end it all: *Dear Jack, Thank you for everything, but I need to be with my family. Goodbye.* She left a note for Jack, went in the kitchen and got the largest knife in the drawer and slashed her wrists very deep to make sure it would work. She bled profusely, and fell to the floor as she was losing consciousness. It would have taken just a few minutes for her to die had it not been for Jack who walked in just in the nick of time to tie her wounds and call 911.

She was rushed to Mt. Pleasant hospital. Following three hours of surgery and ten bags of blood transfusion, she was stable enough to be admitted to the psychiatric ward.

"Why did you save me, why? I want to see my daughter. Please let me go, please." She refused to eat and drink. She was tied in bed in a four-point restraint to keep her from pulling out the intravenous fluid that nourished her. She refused antidepressant medication.

"We'll have to give her ECT," said her treating psychiatrist.

"Did you get hold of any family members?" asked the doctor, hoping to get family permission for the ECT.

"No Doctor, we don't have any contact information."

"We'll have to get a court order then."

The judge granted permission for the procedure after hearing the case.

After the third ECT session, Helen was getting better. She agreed to eat and drink.

"Welcome back Helen, we almost lost you," said the morning nurse.

"What day is it?"

"It's Tuesday," said the nurse, while removing the intravenous tube.

The doctor walked in. "Good morning. Oh you look much better. I'm glad to see you eating." Then he added, "We'd like to get a lot of information from you and I want to discuss starting you on some medications for depression."

"When can I leave?"

"Not any time soon. You almost killed yourself and we want to make sure that you're safe. It's going to take some time for the treatment to work."

The therapist on the team walked in later. "Hi, my name is Grace. I'm the therapist on the team here. We need to talk and we need some information from you. Do you feel like talking now?"

Helen pointed towards the chair next to her bed for Grace to sit down.

"That is how I ended up here the first time. From Mt. Pleasant hospital, they sent me straight to the state hospital, then to here. I got my disability check and I went back to live with Jack," Helen explained to Dr. Oliver.

"What happened to your son? Do you ever wonder?" asked Dr. Oliver.

"Every single day … I saw him once, I don't remember when, but it was on his birthday. I went to Columbia, Jack took me there. He kept pushing me to go see my family. Finally, I gave in. I saw Bobby leaving my mother's house with a beautiful girl. He looked very handsome and happy. He looked exactly like his Dad. He must have been 17 or 18, I lost track. I saw my mom through the window sitting by the fireplace holding my picture. My heart was broken. I almost went in. Jack kept telling me 'Go Helen!' but I couldn't. I was ashamed of the way I looked and of what I'd become. I didn't want him to know his mother was crazy. After all these years, I wasn't sure how he would react. I didn't want to complicate his life. I thought it was better to just leave things the way they were. So I went back to Virginia and I never went back to see my family."

Dr. Oliver was crying. She was feeling nervous trying to summon the courage and to tell her mother-in-law what she knew. Should she tell her now or later? She was not sure what impact the information would have on Helen. Would she run away again? Should she ask to go home with her and tell her there?

She needed consultation on this: there could also be legal ramifications. She walked to Mike's office.

"Mike I need to talk to you."

"Sure, come in."

"This is going to take some time."

Mike looked at his watch and called the front desk. "Ok, my four o'clock has cancelled, have a seat."

She told him everything.

"Are you sure about this? Does Bob know?"

"I'm dead sure. He's called me ten times today, but I haven't called him yet."

"Why don't you talk with your husband and I'll talk to Mrs. Jones? Where is she?"

"She's at the day program, in the back."

"Ok, let's regroup in half an hour."

Mike was a very good and likeable leader. He had that wisdom that some leaders tend to have: partly genetic, partly upbringing and years of experience. He knew the mental health system by heart. He thought he had seen it all, but this had to be a first for him, or for anyone in the system for that matter. He considered how best to tackle this as he walked to the back of the building where the patients gathered to cook their dinner at the day program. He usually walked fast, but this time his pace slowed considerably. He needed time to think this one through.

"Bob where are you?" Dr. Oliver asked her husband on the phone.

"I'm out here in the parking lot. I almost walked in your office. I can't take the wait any longer - is she or isn't she my mother?"

"Ok, I'm coming out."

Dr. Oliver suggested they walk to the nearby coffee shop.

"She *is* your mother," she said.

It was like Bob was zapped by a taser. With this news, on top of the ten cups of coffee he had consumed waiting for his wife, he looked like he was about to have a seizure. He immediately burst into tears.

"Where is she? I want to see her."

"Wait! It isn't that simple. She's bipolar and we have to be careful how we break the news to her. We've no idea how she might react: she may run away again, or have a relapse."

"So what are you suggesting? You're the professional."

"Mike is talking to her now and he'll tell us how to best approach this. I'm in the middle of it and I can't think straight. Meanwhile, do you want to hear what she told me?"

Bob seemed to relax, knowing that there was a plan in place and that he was going to see his mother finally.

10

Reunited

"Mrs. Jones, I have very important information about your son and your family. Do you want to hear it?" Said Mike.

Helen was quiet.

"They've been looking for you for years and they are very anxious to see you and reconnect with you. I asked them to let me talk to you first before they do. Do you want to know about your son and what happened to your mother?"

"My mother?" said Helen.

"Yes, and your son Bob."

"Bobby? Where are they?"

"Well, Bobby is here. He's waiting to see you."

"He's here? No, not like this. Not here. I don't want him to know he has a crazy mother."

"Ok, relax. He's not here at the center. I meant he lives in the area - ten minutes away from the center," said Mike.

"Really? He lives here? Yeah, I want to see him – let's go!" She stood up ready to go.

"Wait. There's more important information. He's married to your doctor."

Helen sat back in the chair and couldn't believe her ears. "Dr. Oliver is ..."

"Yep! She's your daughter-in-law."

"Are you crazy? You've been talking to crazy people all your life, you've become crazy too!"

Mike laughed. "No, it's the truth. I suggest that we all go to Dr. Oliver's house so you can meet your family."

"Ok," agreed Helen.

"Ok, I told her and it went very well - better than I expected. She's very excited and wants to meet Bob. I suggested that we all go to your house and talk," said Mike on the phone, to the very nervous Dr. Oliver.

"Ok great. How?"

"I'll bring her and meet you at your house in twenty minutes."

"Great, we're on the way."

"Bobby my baby, Bobby oh how I missed you!" said Helen, on seeing her son for the first time in thirty years.

"Mom," said Bobby.

They hugged each other and started crying.

"Oh Mom, I missed you so, so much. I can't believe that we're finally united," Bob said in a breaking voice, with tears dripping on his mother's shoulder.

"Forgive me Bobby. I didn't mean to leave you. I didn't know what I was doing or where I was going. I was lost for so long, but I'm so glad I found you. You are the love of my life."

Helen tried to break loose from her son's hug to take a look at him, but couldn't.

Melissa was crying next to them while caressing her mother-in-law's hair. Mike was standing in the background. He waited for few minutes, as he was not sure how things were going to go. But once he felt it was going to be ok, he waved his hand to signal he was leaving.

"Have a seat Helen," said Melissa, as she went to bring some drinks.

"Mom, I heard everything you told Melissa. I guess you want to hear about what happened to me?" said Bob.

Helen nodded.

"Grandma came to New York after the accident. She looked everywhere for you. She called every hospital in New York but couldn't find you, so she took me and went back home. I grew up in the same house you grew up in. I actually had your room. I even went to the same schools you went to. Grandpa died of cancer years ago. Uncle Jack and Uncle Pete both got married. They each have two children. They got jobs out of state and left South Carolina. So it was my grandma and me alone in that big house for a very long time. We had your paintings and Dad's paintings all over the house. They made us feel you were still with us."

At this moment, Helen wept again. Bob, who was already holding his mother's hand, paused and caressed her hand.

"The family would get together for Thanksgiving and Christmas at Grandma's house. We always talked about you, shared stories about your early paintings. By the way, they all still have these portraits - you painted them a long time ago."

Helen laughed as she remembered how funny her first attempts were. "Portraits weren't my strongest thing till I finished art school, I know!"

"In the summer, the whole family would get together at Pawleys Island."

Helen had a big smile on her face, feeling happy that her son got to experience a lot of the things she loved and cherished. The fact that he lived in her room sent chills down her spine. She stared at her son's face, in amazement and gratitude. Even though she had not been there to take son to her favorite places, somehow he still went there.

"I went to college at USC like you and my uncles," said Bob.

"He's a big shot lawyer at one of the biggest firms in DC," added Melissa.

"How did you both meet?"

They looked at each other, waiting to see who was going to speak first.

"I went to medical school at USC. Bob and I met when I took a course in forensic psychiatry that Mr. Hotshot Lawyer here gave. It was love at first sight."

"I know how that goes. So you married your teacher too?"

"Bob asked me out."

"And she said, 'Sure, when?'" said Bob.

They all shared a laugh.

"Any children?"

"No children," said Bob, with a hint of pain on his face that he tried to conceal. "We tried for years but no luck. Who knows, maybe it will happen some day?"

"Anyway we dated for a while before he proposed."

"And again, she said, 'sure'." Bob ducked a flying pillow that Melissa threw at him.

"Our wedding was amazing. Grandmother said, 'I really want to take my time with your wedding Bobby'. I didn't know what she meant, but I understood it later when I heard about her wedding and yours."

"Oh our wedding was fabulous," said Melissa, opening their wedding album to show Helen their photos.

"Oh you got married in Pawleys."

"Yes it is our most favorite place on earth."

"I had my honeymoon there but ... " said Helen.

"I know," said Melissa, who held Helen's hand remembering what had happened during her honeymoon.

Helen was looking around at all the paintings on the walls. She had so many flashbacks looking at them. She stood in front of her mother's portrait for a while, crying, remembering this beautiful painting that kept her from trying to paint her mother because she never thought she could do a better job.

Bob was standing behind her.

"There's something else you need to know, Mom."

Dr. Oliver guessed that he was about to reveal who her real father was. She signaled to him not say anything. She thought that the timing was not the best. So he did not say anything. But Helen was totally absorbed in the paintings and in the flashbacks she was experiencing, so she had not even heard her son.

After the house tour everyone was exhausted, but relieved that it had gone well. But they needed to talk about the here and now. Without any prior planning, Melissa said, "Helen we want you to live with us, this is your home now. No question about it."

"Mom, I want you to be with us: we need to make up for the last forty years," affirmed Bob.

"I don't want to be a burden on you. You know I'm sick and I go through these periods. You have your lives and I don't want to add more stress. Besides, I got used to living alone after Jack died," said Helen. "We'll see each other, but please let me be on my own."

"No Mom, I insist. Let's do a trial for three months. If you're not happy, we'll discuss other arrangements. I want to go with you to South Carolina, to Pawleys. I want to go to

New York to visit our old neighborhood and my Dad's and sister's … " He paused.

Helen started crying again. She wanted to do all this, and doing it with her new family would be all that she could ask or dream for.

Helen moved in. The house was so big. She had her own private suite, with a separate entrance that opened to a beautiful garden in the backyard. She loved gardening, always did, and that was one of the reasons she hated moving to New York. Bob got her an easel, canvases of different sizes and oils, just in case she was in the mood.

Melissa was careful not to be her doctor at home. It was a very difficult balancing act, keeping herself from watching if Helen was taking her medications or getting worried if she heard pacing at night, or if she noticed that Helen was wearing heavy makeup.

Things worked out for the most part. Helen was very cooperative. She wanted to put on her best behavior and knew she needed to take her medication. One time she even told her son, "I am glad you don't have children. I heard in the group today that children can catch this thing. It runs in families."

"I don't care Mom. I love you just the way you are," replied Bobby and gave her a big kiss.

Everyone was so excited about Thanksgiving in Pawleys that year. The news spread that Helen was found and everyone was coming to see her. The whole family and the children all planned to be there. This promised to be the best Thanksgiving ever.

"The car is packed, we're ready to roll," said Bob in excitement to his wife and his mother, rushing them to come down. They all headed to Pawleys Island. Helen looked her best. The new hairdo and clothes made her look her beautiful self again.

"Mom, you look beautiful," said Bob to his mother, who blushed in return.

The rest of the family arrived over the next couple of days. Jack and his family - and Peter and his family, who came from overseas especially to see her.

It couldn't have been better. The cousins, who had not seen each other for a year, were playing games. All the adults were surrounding Helen and catching up, sharing stories about their memories at Pawleys Island. There was so much love and happiness that day.

"This is the best Thanksgiving that we've had since Mom passed away," said Peter.

It was time to eat. Everyone sat at the dining room table. It was time to say thanks. Without exception, everyone was thankful Helen was back and that the family was reunited. It was Helen's turn to say thanks.

After a brief pause, she said, "I don't know why you gave me the mind I have. I don't know how my life would have been if I was normal. I accept it dear Lord, but please don't let anyone else in my family suffer the same. Thank you." She looked at the nieces and nephews in the room. Melissa, who was sitting next to her, held her hand to comfort her. Everyone else looked at her.

"Bless your heart," her sister-in-law said.

After dinner, the guys went to watch the game while the ladies were cleaning the table. Helen walked around and saw the children sitting next to the fireplace reading and playing. The colors and the light were perfect. Something clicked with her and she went looking for the Polaroid camera her son gave her, and snapped a picture. She looked at it, and decided to take another one from a different angle, which she liked better.

She went upstairs looking for something. She looked in all the rooms, but she couldn't find it. Then she climbed up into the attic. She saw it. It was her old easel from way back, from when she came to Pawleys as a child. There were some old tubes of oil, still soft, and her old brushes lying around on a small table next to the easel. She cleaned the easel, taped the photo to the wall and started painting.

"Helen, it is dessert time," called Melissa from downstairs. "You go ahead. I'm full and I need to rest. I'm going to go to sleep," replied Helen who did not want to be interrupted.

Helen died the next morning in the attic. They found her on the floor with a paintbrush in her hand. She had finished the painting of the children that night and was signing it when she gave her last breath. The letter 'S' in Jones was drawn to the edge of the canvas.

*

"We thank you Lord for giving us this precious time to spend with my mother. She suffered a lot during her life, but I know that her last year was a very happy one for her and for us. She'll always be remembered in our hearts and her legacy of art will always be in our family." Bob sat down after giving his eulogy in the small church in George Town, near Pawleys Island.

"I think I'm speaking for everyone here when I say that we're all shocked by my sister's sudden departure. However we're also very happy we got to see her. The thought that we, her family, almost couldn't make it in time, sends chills down my spine. We are so very happy that we were able to make it to see Helen. We would have been devastated had she died and we were not here." Said Peter, he then lifted his head up to the heavens, and with tears in his eyes, said, "So, sister, rest in peace, we love you very much."

The last painting that Helen painted was put on the mantelpiece on top of the fireplace in the house at Pawleys for the whole family to enjoy and share whenever they came. Nobody could have imagined that Thanksgiving would end up this way.

Helen was buried in George Town near Pawleys, instead of the family lot in Columbia. It was a family decision to bury her there, knowing how much she loved the island.

The drive back to Virginia was somber and quiet. Bob broke down in tears every time he looked in the rear-view mirror and did not see his mother. When they finally got home, both were exhausted physically and emotionally so they went straight to bed.

"Bob are you sitting down?" Melissa called Bob few weeks later from her office.

"What, why?" said Bob, starting to panic.

"I think I'm pregnant."

"You think? It's either yes or no."

"Well, I mean I am. The test is positive. Actually, three tests are positive. So I think I'm sure. I should be right?" she said excitedly.

"Yes, yes, I think you are most probably, with the highest degree of certainty, pregnant!"

Helen was born nine months later: a beautiful healthy seven pounds baby.

"Oh God Bob, she looks exactly like your mother," said Melissa.

"She does," said the very happy dad.

Printed in the United States
By Bookmasters